Sin Creek

Susan Whitfield

Cover Design by Linda Houle

This is a work of fiction, and is produced from the author's imagination. People, places and things mentioned in this novel are used in a fictional manner.

ISBN: 978-0-9960683-5-2 (Trade paperback)
ISBN: 978-0-9960683-6-9 (eBook Edition)

Published in the United States of America

Smashwords Edition, License Notes

Published by Studebaker Press

Dear Reader,

Inspiration for the book you're holding in your hands is based on a repulsive truth I fashioned into fiction to raise awareness about the seamy side of some young lives, and the monetary lures that plunge far too many into Internet notoriety, terminal disease, and sometimes, violent death.

When I was a high school administrator, I asked a student of mine how her sister coped with college life. She told me her sister found a lucrative way to raise tuition and live "the high life." What this student said next left me shaken, and I've never been quite the same since.

I went home that night and searched for information the student had casually given me, hoping to find no truth in what she said. I couldn't have been more wrong! I still shiver that some among us are so willing to be part of the filthy underbelly that runs beneath many of our towns and cities.

Research for this book challenged me to search my soul, and I stopped on many occasions not certain if I should continue. But someone needs to tell this story—as ugly and offensive as it may be.

SIN CREEK is truly a work of fiction. However, the seed that started it is alive and spreading like a lethal dose of poison throughout society.

WARNING! This book contains sexually graphic scenes!

It is not meant to offend but to inform.

"Porn is a multi-billion dollar business in the USA."

(Source: www.pbs.org/wgbh/pages/frontline/shows/porn)

"Five million new cases of STDs surface every year in the USA alone."

(Source: www.medicineclinic.org)

"340 million new cases of STDs worldwide."

(Source: The Daily Beast)

Acknowledgements

So many of the same folks have been involved with all my books, so many that it's difficult to list you all individually. Know that I count you among my dearest friends and I sincerely appreciate the tremendous support from each of you.

Thank you so much fellow North Carolina mystery writer, Bill Benners, for the use of a phrase from your novel, *My Sister's Keeper*. It was a perfect introduction to the book.

Special thanks to Peggy and Claude Turner, owners of the inspirational hidden gem, The Green River Bed and Breakfast in Polk County, North Carolina, for providing grape vineyard history and information for this particular book, and for being such wonderful hosts when I visit.

Once again I acknowledge the technical expertise of my friend, Mary Daly, without whose assistance this story never would have been printed.

As always, I must acknowledge the most wonderful family any human could have for their constant love and support.

Life is a journey of chance and choices;
a maze of paths, each leading to a different adventure
and each holding lessons to be learned through pain and
consequence.

~Bill Benners, author of *My Sister's Keeper*

1

I drove to 6150 Rock Creek Road in Brunswick County dressed in the silk and heels I'd worn to my bridal-shower tea. I followed a University of North Carolina-Wilmington campus policeman down Loblolly Loop Trail and through the university's Ev-Henwood Nature Preserve. We passed a pond covered with duckweed, and I thought I saw a gator hump with beady eyes watching me. We arrived at the crime scene where officers from New Hanover and Brunswick counties collected evidence.

I badged my way around some blood and over to the body—white female, badly beaten, unclothed—with only a small amount of mulch covering her emaciated body, her only attire a red leather choke collar with a red heart pendant. Her lower extremities—the groin area specifically—had been shredded by some kind of razor-sharp instrument.

"Agent Hunter," a Brunswick County badge with the name Blake said with a nod. His cell rang before I responded. "Excuse me, ma'am." He turned and answered. "Blake. Go ahead." He listened and nodded while I took a closer look at the crime scene. "That's a positive," I heard him say, "she's pretty torn up in the groin. Yeah, sick bastards." Blake snapped the cell cover shut to end the call and stepped toward me.

"Seems some kid out jogging reported a large amount of blood over by the dorms on the UNCW main campus."

"Killed there and moved here," I said.

"Yes'm." His cell rang again. "Yeah?" I waited again for more information. When this call ended, Blake looked me in the eye.

"They found a small purse not far from all the blood. Purse belongs to a Maeve Smoltz. Had a UNCW freshman ID. Probably one and the same." I moved closer to the dead girl. "They may have found the murder weapon over there too, Agent Hunter."

"Great."

"Not so great for her. A bloody Sawzall," Blake said.

"What's a Sawzall?"

"It's a carpentry tool. I have one myself. It's got different tips, depending on what kind of woodworking project you're doing, but who in his right mind would use it on a person?"

"I think it's reasonable to say whoever did this is not in his right mind, Sergeant Blake."

"Yes, ma'am. You're right. I guess that goes without saying."

"Are there any witnesses here or at main campus?"

"No. This place here is open from dawn to dusk seven days a week, but the Grounds Manager," he glanced at his notes, "a Mr. Tom Barnes, says it's been slow traffic since the semester ended. Want my theory, Agent Hunter?"

"Sure."

"I think the perp killed her on the university campus, came up one of the logging trails at Town Creek, and dumped her out here."

"This is certainly a desolate area," I said, seeing nothing but tall pine trees around me, "but a long way from the university."

A young New Hanover County law-enforcement officer working the crime grid walked up.

"I guess I should be looking for a dildo, but so far—"

"Excuse me?" I stared at him.

"I've heard hardcore crowds use a Sawzall with a dildo, but there's no dildo here," the officer said. "Probably where the saw is."

"You're kidding, right? People use these things for sex?"

"Yes, more than you can imagine. Pretty desperate, huh?"

I couldn't comprehend a saw used for sex, and whoever did this either didn't know what he was doing, or intentionally left a dildo off. I shook my head, hoping the coroner would determine Maeve Smoltz died before this atrocity. What had she done to have her young life end this way?

~~~~~

When I arrived at the Wilmington Police Department on McRae Street, the chief briefed me on their depressing situation. With six unsolved murders in four months on their own docket, I learned I wasn't going to get much—if any—assistance, through no fault of their own. Just an unusual and unfortunate circumstance. They didn't have the luxury of focusing on one case. That left me—and a small group of SBI agents who would probably pop in and out—to solve Maeve Smoltz's murder.

Governor Bev Perdue had recently held a press conference about the state's economic crisis and her budget cuts, creating a situation where all law-enforcement entities became short-staffed. Positions arising from retirements and resignations were left unfilled from local to state levels, all a direct result of the national and international financial mess that affected all of us. To make matters worse, the feds, who usually had a hard-on for porn—no pun intended—now had a new top priority. Since the recent discovery of a terrorist cell living and operating in North Carolina, terrorism on American soil had become a primary focal point, and that involved plenty of SBI agents. If that weren't enough, the state planned to release rapists and murderers back into society due to overcrowded prisons. I had an answer for that one, but nobody wanted to reinstate capital punishment.

I sucked in the humidity and slammed the Hummer door a little harder than necessary, frustration attaching itself to me like a second skin. I grew up in humidity. Why then, had I never become accustomed to it? My mood soured more as I thought about the way Maeve Smoltz died.

2

I waited at the morgue for Dr. and Mrs. Dilwith Smoltz to identify the body of their daughter. Tina Smoltz, a New Hanover Regional Medical Center nurse was short and stout, with bangs and shoulder-length dark locks that turned under, and Dr. Smoltz, with graying blond hair, a college professor. Maeve resembled him.

I hated to watch the one sliver of parents' hope dissipate as the sheet lifted back far enough to reveal the face they loved, dissolving the tomb quiet into uncontrollable sobs. The coroner, Burl Legassie, quickly covered Maeve. As the parents walked out, he pulled me to the side.

"An interesting discovery during the preliminary, Agent Hunter. I'm seeing more and more of this stuff. May mean something. May not."

"What's that?"

"Her outer labia is pierced even though detached from the torso. Her genitals were in a separate bag, you know."

I nodded, having heard the mangled flesh had been found on the university campus and still finding it difficult to comprehend. I wouldn't have expected this innocent-

looking girl to be pierced *there,* even though I went to school
with plenty of girls who claimed to have piercings in places
I would never consider. My ears would do just fine. I had
no plans to pierce any other body parts.

Legassie continued, "She was undoubtedly sexually
active with plenty of scar tissue around the vagina and anus."

"Could she have been raped?"

"It's unlikely. I think she's been active for some time.
Probably some rough sex, but not a one-time incident. I'll
do my best to collect semen and other trace and call you,
but you do realize she's cut to pieces there. First case of
female circumcision I've actually seen in my career." He
shook his head.

"Thanks for the information," I found myself
whispering. "And thank you for just uncovering her face."

"I seldom reveal more than that unless the face is
unrecognizable. Then we have to search for a birthmark,
tat, or some identifier a family member knows about. There's
no need to put this girl's parents through that kind of agony."

I agreed.

I hurried to catch up with Maeve's parents getting into
their Buick Regal. "Dr. and Mrs. Smoltz, I'm truly sorry for
your loss. I just wanted to let you know that our department
will have many tough questions while we're investigating
her death. Be prepared for a visit. And please let us know
what we can do to help you through this."

Maeve's father's face twitched as he nodded and closed
the passenger door for his wife.

~~~~~

Shade trees on Martin Street sheltered folks from the
heat as they beat a path to 386, the Smoltz residence, a
modest gray brick house with dark red shutters. I got in line
and moved along with others, entering the front door with

its oval glass inset, and trying to listen in on whispers and conversations about the deceased. I signed the guest book and searched for Maeve's parents, trying to ignore a terrier, barking nonstop at the strangers who invaded his house. I maneuvered around a dining table and chairs in a room that seemed more appropriate for a library, bookcases and shelves from floor to ceiling embracing the single window. I studied a buffet lamp: seven teapots stacked one atop the other.

I peeked around the corner at Dilwith Smoltz standing at a bar in a kitchen the color of lemon zest, sipping coffee and talking quietly, hugging friends who approached with casseroles and condolences. I diverted my eyes, spotting blue and pink teapot bookends holding cookbooks. I liked the bright kitchen with its white cabinetry and stainless appliances, including a large pot rack over the center island. It had probably been a happy place until now.

Tina Smoltz sobbed in a gazebo out back with a number of ladies who were, no doubt, trying to comfort her. While I hated this part of my job, I started out the back door, but Dilwith Smoltz gently tugged my arm.

"Agent Hunter, can we talk?"

I nodded and stepped back in.

"Coffee?"

"Yes, I believe I will. Thanks."

He poured and I added cream and sugar before following him down a narrow hall. "I'm sorry to intrude at such a difficult time."

"I understand the need. My wife…well, I'd rather you ask me questions for now, Agent Hunter. She's hysterical." We turned into a small disorganized office.

"I'm sure it's horrible for both of you. Do you have any more children?"

"No, Maeve's our only baby, and spoiled rotten. But Tina had several miscarriages over the years." His sad eyes met mine. "We'd give our lives to have her back, Agent Hunter."

"I'm sure you would, sir." I sipped my coffee. "I could use your help."

"Anything, Agent Hunter. What can I do?"

"I need a list of all her friends, anyone she associated with or mentioned. Even one time. Do you know of any person who disliked her or threatened her?"

"I can't think straight right now, but my wife and I'll put together a list of friends. You know she lived in a condo off campus, so I don't know everybody she associated with. Her roommate might be helpful, but I can't remember her name right this minute."

"Antonella Beaujue-Dufour?"

"That's it. Have you talked with her?"

"Not yet, but she's the only name on my list right now, so I'll be visiting her shortly."

"She should know something." He ducked his head for a second and looked at me again. "Maeve's never mentioned being threatened, and I really think she'd have told me if anything like that happened. She loved UNCW and never complained about any problems at all. We're at a loss. I can't comprehend this. Maeve was a quiet girl." His eyes watered. "You know they say that monster shredded her in the—"

"Who told you that?"

"Somebody who dropped by the house. You know, they all mean well, but they love to gossip. In truth, I overheard it. Is that true, Agent Hunter?"

"Listen, Dr. Smoltz—"

"Is it true, Agent Hunter?" His voice was a mixture of anger and sorrow.

"I'm afraid so, sir. Try not to think about that." *Easy for me to say.* I gave him a minute to compose himself. "She never brought any friends here to the house?"

"Not since high school days."

"Did you ever take her out with a couple of friends along?"

"No, Agent Hunter. Like I said, she was pretty much a loner, I suppose."

"I'd like to drop by tomorrow for that list, Dr. Smoltz, even if it's short. She may have known her killer."

He shuddered noticeably.

"Does she have a room here with some of her things?"

"Yes, of course. Would you like to see it?"

"Absolutely."

"Follow me."

He led me down a short hallway and opened the white room decorated with painted furniture the color of cobalt. The sheer red print curtains complemented the folded quilt at the end of the bed. The room looked more like a child's room than one belonging to a college student. The professor walked over to a small white desk with a blue chair.

"She used this when she came home. We bought her a laptop and this table was a good size for it." He peered out the only window, his back to me, and blew his nose.

"I see another teapot lamp." I hoped to lighten the mood.

"Yes, Tina, my wife, is obsessed with teapots. You'll find them all over this house. I can't say much because you'll also find plenty of ceramic dogs all over the place."

I smiled. "Dr. Smoltz, we'll need to go through this room to see if there are any clues to her murder. Not even you and your wife should touch anything. Items here and in her apartment will be collected, including her computers. We want to know whom she connected with on the Internet. Her assailant could be a predator in cyberspace. Lord knows there're plenty of them out there."

I cordoned off the doorframe and he locked the door and dropped the key in my hand.

"Did Maeve have a job?"

"She worked at Campus Canteen a few hours a week. That's the only place she ever mentioned hanging out. We paid for everything. We wanted her to concentrate on her studies so even during this recession, Tina and I made whatever sacrifices were necessary to give her what she needed. We were lucky she found a roommate in that condo or we couldn't afford that kind of luxury. Antonella's mother is a real estate agent. Even though she could afford for her to live alone, she didn't want her to for some reason. Quite fortunate for us."

I'm not so sure about that. "Thank you for your time, Mr. Smoltz."

He nodded and we headed back toward the kitchen.

I found the front entrance and excused myself as Dr. Smoltz joined people crowded into every room of the house.

As I headed for the Hummer, I saw a beautiful young woman walking up the sidewalk. She glanced at me and sped up the steps with some other people, speaking with a soft French accent. I moved in her direction, causing her to hesitate and turn toward me. She wore dark wrap-around shades.

"Are you Antonella?"

"Yeah. Uh, yes, I am."

"I'm Agent Logan Hunter. SBI," I said, not showing my badge.

"I can't talk to you."

"I understand this is not a good time, but I have to ask you some questions about Maeve. I have your address. I'll be dropping by."

The girl mashed her sunglasses tighter to her face and said nothing.

I got closer so that she knew I could see the black eye anyway. "Take care of yourself."

I ambled down the sidewalk, almost bumping into a nasty-looking guy with uncombed hair in his eyes and black whiskers that went from sideburn to sideburn and down to his grossly protruding Adam's apple. The shadow of a black mustache curved across disgusting lips. He was, perhaps, the most vulgar-looking man I'd ever seen. He sneered at me when I passed.

Once I got into the Hummer, I watched Puke Face arguing with Antonella. I wanted to hear the conversation but too much distance foiled that idea. I eased out of my spot on the street and put the window down. As I approached, he looked toward me, made some final comment to her, and walked away. Apparently he hadn't come to give condolences to the Smoltzes.

I circled the block, hoping to see him again or maybe get another chance to corner Antonella. I struck out.

3

I thrust my badge at the brunette with two bruised eyes when she opened her condominium door. As I looked at Antonella Beaujue-Dufour's face, more questions came to mind for the petite college junior standing in front of me.

"Agent Hunter?"

She walked to a fuchsia couch and collapsed. I closed the door behind me.

"Miss Beaujue-Dufour, I need to ask you some questions about Maeve Smoltz."

"Why? What did she do?"

"You're aware she was murdered. I saw you at the Smoltzes' house."

"I remember."

She grabbed several bright couch pillows and hugged them to her chest, her rosy skin losing its color.

I walked over and looked down at the young woman cowering like a scared pup behind her cushions. "You don't seem to be doing too well yourself. Do you want to tell me about your black eyes?"

She whimpered a weak "no".

"Were you and Maeve close?"

"Not really. I mean, we did a few things together, but we aren't really much alike." I picked up a little of her French accent now.

"Whom did she hang around with? Male and female."

She would no longer make eye contact with me. "I really don't know."

"Surely if you lived with this girl you know some of her friends."

She sat up a little, but said nothing, shaking her head slowly.

"Look, this is a murder investigation. I need your help."

"I already told you. I didn't know her at all before she moved in here. I didn't socialize with her. She never had friends over here like I did. The only reason I'm living with her is because I'm being punished."

"Punished by whom?"

"My mom." She turned red. "She thinks she's teaching me a lesson. Look, I've said too much. I'm just shocked is all."

"Did your mom give you the black eyes?"

"No! Of course not! No, she's just punishing me to teach me a lesson about money. Otherwise I'd be living in my own place on the beach or the Cape Fear River by myself."

"What about the guy you argued with at the Smoltz house?"

"We weren't arguing. I just don't like him."

"Okay. I'll let that go for now, but while I'm here I need to get into Maeve's room and collect her belongings and anything that might help find her killer."

She pointed a trembling finger around the corner.

I searched Maeve's personal belongings after disconnecting and loading her computer into my Hummer. She had an impressive and contradictory stash of clothes and accessories for such a young person. As I pulled out items, I labeled and bagged them. Suede knee-high boots still had the $149 price tag attached. A Miss Tina cage purse, a $250 tag still intact. A Prada bag? That had to set her back at least $800. And Jimmy Choo shoes well over a grand.

I pulled out a closet drawer and found gel-filled falsies, several lace Vikinis, and a 32A bustier. I lifted a few hangers, some holding child-like clothing: a yellow baby-doll halter dress and a polka-dot baby-doll dress. A pink hoodie mini dress and a size two low-cut red sweater dress were anything but child-like. A hot pink ruched dress, neckline cut to the waist, and a plaid corset dress looked like street-corner attire.

Maeve's roomie appeared in the doorway. "Can I get the things I loaned her?"

"Not right now. Just make me a list of what's yours."

She disappeared in a huff.

Once I'd gathered everything I thought necessary, I cordoned off the room and pulled out a card and laid it on the table in front of Antonella. "If you think of anything, please get in touch with us. And, Ms. Beaujue-Dufour, don't plan on taking any trips."

"Are you telling me I'm a suspect?"

"Everybody's a suspect at this time."

4

I got a short list of names from Dilwith Smoltz and his wife. It primarily contained neighborhood friends and young people from their church. They couldn't give much information about college acquaintances.

"She wanted to be independent, you know," Tina Smoltz said. "She didn't want us prying into her business. Now I wish we had."

She dissolved into tears. Most, but not all, of their list had names and contact information they'd pieced together to help me. I got details about the funeral service and left, hoping to make some contacts before dark.

~~~~~

I started with Antonella again. I wanted to learn more about the nasty guy who obviously made her uncomfortable. Had he given her the black eyes? And why confront her outside the Smoltz house?

"Agent Hunter, I'm on my way out."

"That's odd. You just came in."

"Are you following me?"

"Miss Beaujue-Dufour, I'm not taking any flak from you. I'm investigating the death of your roommate. You might try being a little more cooperative. Obstructing justice is a serious crime."

This remark seemed to surprise her, and she opened the door for me to enter.

"I see you've abandoned the sun shades."

She nodded and offered me a seat.

"Miss Beaujue-Dufour, I'll get right to the point. When I left the Smoltzes' house, I literally bumped into a guy, black hair, kind of gross...arguing with you."

"Uh, yeah. That's Rude."

"I'll buy that."

"No, I mean, everybody calls him Rude. His real name is Rudd, Rudd Roache."

What an appropriate name for a disgusting-looking man. "At first I thought he was on his way to see the Smoltz family, but I couldn't help noticing he talked to you and you didn't seem too happy about it. And he left without visiting Maeve's parents. I've asked you about this before." Her rosy cheeks paled. "How do you know him?"

"He's just a guy."

"Who is he and what's your relationship with him?"

Antonella threw a pillow on the floor. "I don't have a relationship with that nasty turd!"

"So how does he know you?"

"He's just a guy, okay? He hangs around doing...uh, mostly nothing. He's always trying to put the move on any girl he sees. He's a sorry-ass dropout. He started out majoring in technology and web design. He said he dropped out because he knew ten times more than any of his professors. He's always telling everybody his IQ is at the genius level, but he's still a turd."

"Did he hang around Maeve?"

"I don't know. I really can't help you with this, Agent Hunter. Please stop coming here."

"Antonella, did this Rude threaten you? Did he hit you?"

"I'm a klutz. Nobody's hit me or threatened me."

Somehow her French-accented words weren't convincing.

5

I hurried through the back door of the Genesis Beach First Baptist Church, carefully scrunching my wedding gown bag enough to get inside, with my dear friend, Taryn Kosterman, close behind me with my satin shoes and bouquet. I only had one hour to get ready for my marriage to Chase Railey, the love of my life.

Relaxed but excited, we decided to marry at the beach even though Chase's mother, Fern, would have been better off staying near her home in Asheville. We offered to have the wedding there, but she insisted that a bride should be married near her home. Fern battled cancer, rapidly losing the fight, but she attended the wedding, driven the eight hours by her loyal butler, Clive, and making the trip across the state a two-day journey with plenty of time to rest.

Chase and I worried the trip would be too much for her, but Fern insisted she wouldn't miss her only child's wedding to a woman who had won her approval. I stood still for a second at the thought of Fern sitting on the front pew alone, my mother having died a few months before this special day. Chase's father, Drew, was in jail and mine died when I was a child. I wiped a tear and promised myself only happy thoughts on the most special day of my life.

I peeked out a window toward the beach where my pal, Pepper, delegated assignments to her wait staff to set up the reception in a huge white party tent on the ocean side of the sand dunes. She made the wedding cakes and all buffet food while Taryn, the artist, decorated tables and arranged church flowers, luscious ferns, and my bouquet.

"Come on, Logan. Time's a-wasting!"

Taryn unzipped the bag and I dropped my jeans and shirt in a pile on the tiled floor.

"You and Pepper picked out a gorgeous gown, Logan." She gave me a peck on the cheek. "You'll be the most beautiful bride ever!"

Taryn, Pepper, and I had melded into what Chase called "the trio." Where you found one, you found all—except, of course, when our unique schedules pulled us apart. Pepper's restaurant in Cary kept her busy, and Taryn lived in Luck, on the other side of the state, teaching art and selling her homemade wares at festivals and fairs. That didn't keep us from talking every day and we were there for each other when needed. SBI assignments required me to move around the state wherever criminal investigations carried me, and that's how I'd met all three of them.

"You're a lucky lady, marrying the hunk of western North Carolina."

"Don't I know it, but don't let Chase hear you say that. I won't be able to put up with him."

Taryn checked her watch. "Well, in less than forty-five minutes, he's yours for life."

I grinned.

"Geez! Help me into the gown, Taryn, and then we'll do my face and hair." I'd already put on a special enhancer bra that made me look as though I had breasts. I stepped into the strapless gown and pulled it up. The bra made the ivory gown's bodice with Swarovski crystals stunning. The hi-low hem suited a beach wedding and reception in the sand. Taryn tightened the satin-ribbon corset back with a grunt.

"Taryn, I can't breathe!"

"I want that tiny waist to be noticed, Logan. After you have a brood of children, it'll never be the same."

I laughed. "A brood? I don't think so. Anyway, I want to be comfortable and able to say my vows. Loosen it a bit." She pulled ribbons away from my body a little. "And I'm not planning to have children any time soon. Chase and I aren't together enough as it is, and we need time before we consider adding children to the chaos."

Taryn covered the knife scar at my throat and the bullet scar on my shoulder with compound that matched my skin tone. Then we completed my makeup and turned our attention to my short blond hair. I decided to forego headgear, opting instead to pin in a couple of rosebuds and hope a gust of beach breeze didn't rip them out.

"You know there's a possibility of a thunderstorm," I said.

"I'm ready if it rains." I must have looked confused. "Never you mind. I've got it covered."

She did a final inspection and handed me the bouquet she made of Calla lilies and orchids in shades of white, purple, fuchsia, and lime green.

"I absolutely love this bouquet."

"I'm so glad, darlin'."

We entered a long hall that led to the sanctuary and heard the music Chase and I had selected together.

"I only wish Cecilia could sing for you and Chase today."

Taryn read my mind. Cecilia Nesbitt, a close friend of Taryn's, was one of the victims of a serial killer on a case I'd investigated in the mountains. I had the privilege of hearing her sing at another victim's funeral, having no idea that she would later become a victim herself.

A hard shower erupted and Taryn left me standing in the hallway, grabbed a jar from a nearby table, and ran out into the rain.

Not another hot flash! Not now, for crying out loud!

I watched through a church window as she filled the jar with rain, shaking my head in disbelief.

Sometimes I think that woman's britches are twisted up too tight in the crotch!

Taryn raced back to me as the shower ended as abruptly as it had begun. She tugged me along toward the vestibule.

"Taryn, what in—?"

"Not now, Logan, we don't have time for idle chit-chat." She shook raindrops from her emerald dress.

In front of us a hall door opened and Clive stepped out. I peered around him to see Fern Railey, pale as death, blow me a kiss. She wore a royal purple dress in understated elegance and sat in a wheelchair. Clive pushed the chair to the edge of the carpet. At that point, Fern insisted on abandoning it and walking down the aisle with Clive and Chase to be seated on the right front pew.

As I watched this special gesture, I teared up again, wishing my daddy were alive to walk me down the aisle and give my hand to Chase. As if he knew, Chase's moist eyes met mine. We both smiled and then beamed. He walked back to where I stood—never losing eye contact—and clutched my arm, leading me to the front of the church as everyone attending turned to watch us. We nodded at Ken Poletti, the SBI director, as we passed him.

The ceremony transpired with sweet vows we wrote ourselves, short but sincere:

"You are my Life, my Universe. In our world of lies and deceit, you are my Truth. You are my Candle, my Guiding Light. I will cherish you beyond forever."

We posed for pictures, hearing about the ice sculpture, its two entwined hands of ice broken during transfer from the church chiller to the reception tent. Someone said "Bad omen!" loud enough for us to hear, but Chase and I kissed and snickered to declare that the mishap would not spoil our special day. Ice would have melted quickly in the Carolina heat anyway.

We were fortunate to have such a beautiful day in early May when it usually rained, but North Carolina's severe drought kept significant rain away once again, and the one quick shower didn't dampen our spirits. We reveled at the opportunity to have the reception outside. Everywhere my eyes went I saw lovely flowers and tablescapes Taryn arranged, right down to sea star photo frames used for nameplates.

Chase and I, both famished, filled our plates with sugar-cured ham, boiled shrimp, Grand Marnier chicken, and an array of salads, fruits, and vegetables before sitting in chairs Taryn had covered with white linen. The crowd of sixty couldn't possibly consume all the food Pepper had prepared. Wine and beer flowed, and no one left early. A beach band played while many de-shoed folks shagged in cool sand.

We cut the wedding cake, fashioned after my gown and topped with blown sugar entwined hands, and Chase cut the groom's cake of chocolate ganache edged with huge fresh strawberries dressed in dark and white chocolate tuxedos. Some of both cakes ended up on my plate. I chowed down at the same time I saw my wedding ring hung in my gown. Chase and I gently worked to free the two, somehow breaking a fragile prong from his mother's antique diamond. A hush fell over the head table and spread throughout the tent.

"Oh no! Another bad omen!" the same shithead said too loud.

But Taryn saved the day in the sweetest way. She stood beside us and presented Chase and me with the Mason jar filled with rainwater, now wrapped in ribbon. Everyone looked on with great curiosity.

"Logan and Chase, as you begin your life together, know that we all love you and wish you many happy and healthy years together. And when you have your first child, use this rainwater—which I caught on the first day of your life as husband and wife—to baptize him. The water has been boiled and the jar sealed until that day. May you both be blessed."

Taryn got a standing ovation and I cried. I'd never heard of such a charming gesture, and Chase and I would cherish the gift until we had the opportunity to use it some years down the road.

~~~~~

We postponed our honeymoon trip because of Fern's health, and more crime than our bureau could handle with two agents on leave at the same time. Taryn took Homer, our basset hound, with her to run the hundreds of acres around her mountain home and keep her company. Chase and I would miss the hound, but our jobs weren't conducive to pets of any kind. We knew Taryn would spoil him worse than we had since we adopted him after his owner was killed near Black River during a previous investigation.

Our first night as husband and wife proved to be beyond anything I had ever imagined. It didn't matter that we were at Genesis Beach instead of in the Caribbean. Chase and I, both insatiable, tore up both beds and crinkled up a sofa. But the wildest pleasure came on the kitchen island, under the scrutiny of bright work lights Pepper designed when she owned the condominium.

Back in the master suite, we lay stroking each other's faces and arms while our legs pretzeled around each other. Sweet sexy scents invaded my nostrils and I grinned at Chase, who kissed my nose.

"I'm starved. How about you?"

"I am, but I'm enjoying the moment. Don't move yet."

We snuggled. It felt so right with the man I loved right beside me. I wanted to take it all in, to feel all there was to feel, to touch and be touched in every way humanly possible, to keep these precious moments from ending.

When we finally untangled from one another, I let out a pitiful sigh, reality hitting hard.

"When are you leaving for Asheville?"

"After breakfast."

"Maybe Fern will be better by the time you get there. I'm sorry she had such a rough trip back after the wedding."

Chase poured us both coffee. "Logan, we both know the end is near." I tried to see the bottom of my cup through black liquid. We ate cheese toast in silence, then I straightened the sofa and stripped sheets off both beds while he showered and dressed.

I stood behind him while he combed his wavy hair. I tried to absorb the blond hair, tanzanite eyes, broad shoulders, tight butt. How I loved that man! My husband. A smile raced across my face as the butt in those light khaki pants twitched just before he turned to face me.

"Spying on me, Mrs. Railey?"

"Just checking out the merchandise, mister."

He sauntered over and wrapped me in his arms. "I thought you did a pretty good job of that during the night."

"Have you packed a bag?"

"I'm taking the bag I packed for the honeymoon and a suit and tie. No telling what's in it. Clive will take care of me once I get there."

I walked out with him even though I only wore a gown and panties.

"I'll come as soon as I can," I vowed, giving him a lingering kiss.

My heart clutched watching him drive away, waving at me through his opened window.

6

I always locked my aging Hummer wherever I parked it, day or night. It was a good habit. So I found the piece of pink notebook paper under a wiper blade. The scrawled note indicated a web site, *www.fearsomeferry.com*, maybe an ad to get me to cruise the port city's Cape Fear River on a ferry during the annual Azalea Festival. But the festival had already passed. I wadded up the paper but decided not to be a litterbug. I'd dispose of it later. I hopped in and drove back toward University Towers, hoping to locate a name on the Smoltzes' short list, namely a Bailey Manley. I asked some students about her at the front desk and a couple of them directed me to 419.

No answer. A student passing in the hall said most students had gone home or to summer jobs.

Back in the Hummer, I looked over at the crinkled note, retrieved it, and read it again. *Fearsome Ferry?* I unwrinkled the note and stuck it in my pocket. I'd look it up on the Internet after Maeve's funeral.

~~~~~

I wore a two-piece navy dress, added a string of large pearls, and stepped into stack heel sandals before running my fingers through the hair I'd allowed to get a little too long since Maeve's murder and the wedding. Who had time for a haircut? I'd have to find the time, though, since it grew over my ears and tickled the nape of my neck.

I arrived at Andrews Mortuary on Market Street early and sat on the back left side in order to see everyone who came. Pink flowers of every type imaginable draped over a closed silver casket. Many older folks attended, apparently friends of Tina and Dilwith Smoltz, but I wanted to focus my attention on the younger college crowd who might come to pay last respects.

I had been to many funerals where crowds overflowed into the yard, but not this one. The mammoth chapel felt uncomfortable, the sparse attendants mostly near the front.

After the family entered, a few younger people came in and sat a few pews ahead of me on the right side of the aisle. I nodded at Antonella, dressed in all black, who didn't reciprocate. A pretty light-complexioned girl with wiry hair pulled back behind her ears and a few springy pieces jutting out around her forehead sat beside her. She wore no makeup and no jewelry, only a nutmeg skirt and ivory sweater with embroidery down the front. A handsome young man with thick, dark brown hair came in wearing a gray shirt with dark slacks and sat down beside her. He glanced my way and soon whispered to the two girls.

The service began. I attended far too many memorial services and funerals conducted for victims of some vicious person who didn't value life. Maeve's life had just begun, and it may have been her desire to be independent that got her killed. Several eulogies, songs, and prayers led to the end of the service. I remained standing after the family left, wanting to get a better look at those who attended. Antonella and the wiry-haired girl were somber. The hunk offered me a half smile while passing my pew.

I hoped to talk to a few people after the service, but once outside, they scurried to vehicles as it began to rain. I did, however, notice the nasty guy called Rude—who hadn't attended the service—and the hunk exchange a few words and go separate ways.

Interesting.

I picked up a spinach pizza and headed for home. I had a date with the Internet.

I cranked up my Dell while undressing and eating pizza with extra sauce and cheese. I zipped my denim shorts and threw a clay-dyed tee shirt over my head, grabbed a cold beer, and took the rest of the pizza with me to the computer. I sat down to find out what the scrawled note meant. I typed in *www.fearsomeferry.com* and almost spewed pizza when the screen filled with young naked girls doing unspeakable things right in front of me and millions of other strangers around the world. I squirmed, expecting to be struck by lightning, but my curiosity took control. The site required a credit card fee to view hard-core videos, but I got plenty of information from the free "visitor's tours" I clicked on, including a close pickle shot—full frontal male.

I toggled down the screen, more girls appearing in thumbnails having sex with penises in a variety of sizes and colors. Pizza sauce dripped from my mouth to the keyboard.

"Shit!"

I ran to grab a damp cloth to clean it. I wiped and tried to comprehend what this site might have to do with Maeve's murder, if anything. I slammed the rest of the pizza into the fridge and sat back down with renewed focus, pulling a notepad over in case I wanted to take notes.

I went back to the top of the site's home page, found a link to another site and read bold paragraphs beside it, surrounded by pornographic images. The open letter from the site's owner stated he and a few friends drove around university towns in vans, looking for girls who wanted to make a fast one-thousand-dollar bill. He said he'd been shocked and delighted at how many were willing to do anything for the money. He had them sign a form declaring they were over eighteen and agreed to be filmed having sex with strangers, apparently a lucrative business. He also mentioned taking some of them to a ferry named *Fearsome Ferry* on numerous occasions. The link to *www.flashvan.com*, called "sex on wheels", left me flabbergasted.

I went to thumbnails and clicked on some to enlarge images of girls with their legs in the air, revealing the entire female anatomy in all its glory. Some girls with their mouths stuffed with the most monstrous penises I'd ever seen—not that I'd seen many—some dark brown, resembling logs rather than sex organs. Other pictures showed girls catching spewed semen in their mouths, pumped from a penis whose owner managed to avoid having his identity exposed.

Apparently the same guy owned both the ferry and the van operations. I clicked on the ferry link again around midnight, book marking both sites containing thousands of thumbnails. Then I clicked on The Flash Van site once again and a picture of a psychedelic van, set up with cameras and enough room for filming rowdy sex, filled the screen. No way to go over either site in one sitting, but I'd had all I could take anyway. Disgust washed over me.

My mind reeled. Could innocent-looking Maeve be on either site—or both? Could this be behind her death? And these other girls… Some didn't look anywhere near eighteen. The arrogant letter boasted of thousands of "stupid sluts willing to do anything for money." Unfortunately the Webmaster didn't post any identifying information, but I'd definitely be visiting again. If Maeve Smoltz pointed a lifeless finger at these sites, I'd be looking for the predator behind them with the help of experts in the latest technology and current Internet activities.

7

Around daybreak I typed in the flesh market site, *www.flashvan.com* and launched my official investigation. If Maeve Smoltz was on it, I was determined to find her. The site had thousands of different girls engaging in a wide assortment of sexual acts—a veritable variety store on wheels—with full-face shots and blatant disregard for even the slightest degree of decency.

It didn't take long to find Maeve engaging in different sexual acts with different men—and having a dildo used on her by another girl—several different times over the hours I scoped out thumbnails. The innocent-looking Maeve appeared to be a pro, on the van on many occasions since what few clothes she wore differed in each video stream. There had to be a link between the porn industry and Maeve's murder.

I dreaded going to the Smoltz home again. Maeve's face, along with the rest of her, had been around the world for weeks, possibly months. The Webmaster didn't have enough decency to delete her pictures after she died. I already had enough to sink him—or her—if I could get behind the monitor, but the Webmaster could live anywhere in the world. Getting the scumbag would take more knowledge than I had about the world of the Internet.

~~~~~

Tina and Dilwith Smoltz met me at the door, he with a schnauzer under one arm. We sat at the oak dining table in mahogany chairs that didn't match. A collection of antique teapots sat on some old books, waiting to be put on the room's library shelves. I stole a glance at a framed picture of Maeve in happy times. Dilwith adjusted his chair so he could see me around a bouquet of mixed flowers that filled the middle of the table.

"What have you found out, Agent Hunter?"

I cleared my throat to begin as Tina offered me an apple. I took a big bite, taking my time with the question while I savored its crisp sweetness.

"Dr. and Mrs. Smoltz, I have some difficult things to say. I know your hearts broke the night we went to the morgue. I'm afraid what I'm about to tell you will break your hearts again."

Tina stared and Dilwith readjusted himself in the chair. "Spit it out, Agent Hunter. We've heard a few things. Some people have started avoiding us, like *we* did something wrong. We just want to know. Then we can deal with it."

I had to wonder about that.

"Yes, sir. You already know we confiscated nearly everything in your daughter's two bedrooms—the one here and the one at her condominium—along with her computer, clothes, and other personal effects. We also got her cell phone records to determine who'd called her and whom she had called or texted in the hours before her death." I paused. "Maeve had phone sex—"

Tina Smoltz trembled. "You can't possibly know that!"

"Please honey, let her tell us. Then we'll come to terms with it." Dilwith nodded for me to continue.

"Mrs. Smoltz, we traced over two-hundred 900 calls to her cell phone. She apparently had quite a few regular phone contacts and the calls were lengthy, some as long as forty-five minutes.

"Her computer gave us even more evidence. She had a Web cam at her condo so she could perform for the camera while talking to someone—either on the phone or on the Internet. She had a PayPal account, which allowed her to collect money before committing to clients."

"Then somebody used her phone! And 'clients'? You make her sound like a whore!"

"Tina, please!"

"She had over thirty-thousand dollars in her online bank account, Mrs. Smoltz."

"What?" Both parents were now stunned. Dilwith paced.

"She wanted to take more responsibility for her finances and not lean on us so much. She asked me if she could set up her own bank account. I let her," Dilwith said in anguish. "Oh my God!" He walked over to a window and stared out. Tina froze in place.

"We have technicians going through all the thousands of text messages and incoming credit card accounts to see if she possibly connected with a pedophile. It'll be a while before we have that information." I shuffled toward the door. "Maybe that's all you need to know."

"No. Please continue," Dilwith said with his back turned. "Really. I…we'd rather know than have to hear all the rumors and whispering behind our backs."

"If you're sure, sir." They both nodded. "According to a witness, a couple of men approached Maeve at the college canteen and asked if she'd like to make a quick thousand dollars. From my interviews with the other waitresses who work there, Maeve briefly hesitated, but then said she'd go with them. One of the girls said Maeve begged her to go along, but when she saw that the van, called The Flash Van, had video cameras and enough room to pose, she refused."

Tina's hands were over her mouth as if to stop me from talking. Dilwith gestured for me to go on.

"Maeve apparently went with the men—total strangers—and they later dropped her off with a thousand-dollar bill in her hand. The manager of the canteen—Mr. Ben Green—said the same van picked her up there on several more occasions and she got another thousand-dollar bill each time. After the third ride, she told Mr. Green she wouldn't be working at the canteen anymore; she'd found easier, quicker money."

Dilwith's eyes watered and Tina turned the color of her nurse's uniform.

"Maybe I harped on our financial situation too much, with the economy being in shambles." Dilwith scrubbed his hair. I hoped the economy wouldn't drive more desperate people to pornography.

"I found a crumpled piece of paper on my Hummer one night with *Fearsome Ferry* web site on it. Nothing else. I went home and found the site—all porn. Pretty young girls having sex on film, Maeve included."

"My daughter was a virgin! She's never even had a boyfriend."

"Mrs. Smoltz, I'm not here to break your heart. Really. But according to the medical examiner, her labia, vagina, and anus all had scar tissue," I said as gently as possible, knowing it would hit them like a freight train.

"They raped her? That's what you're saying, isn't it?" Dr. Smoltz leaned over his wife's shoulder, apparently not taking in the full meaning of what I'd been saying. Who could blame them for denial?

"No, I'm sorry to say she appeared to be quite sexually active. Had been for some time, according to the ME."

"Are you saying my daughter's a slut?" I hesitated a little too long. "Well?"

The distraught woman slammed her palms on the table. "These are all lies. Lies! I can't listen to any more of this, Dilwith." She turned her back to me. "Get her out! Get her out of my house this instant!"

Dr. Smoltz tried to put his hands on his wife's shoulders, but she ran from the room, crying hysterically.

"I'm sorry, Dr. Smoltz. I'd better go," I said, looking into his wet eyes.

Dilwith sat down stoically in the chair across from me, not looking in the direction his wife went. "No. Go ahead, Agent Hunter."

"Are you sure?"

"Yes, yes! Get on with it!" He tried unsuccessfully to choke down the sobs. "I have to know the truth!"

"Yes, sir. I'm concerned about you, that's all." I cleared my throat. "I first found videos of Maeve on The Flash Van site."

"They drugged her, didn't they? The bastards drugged and raped my little girl."

"No, sir. I'm sorry. All witnesses say Maeve willingly went with them, signed a paper declaring she was over eighteen when barely seventeen, and agreed to have sex for the money," I repeated.

Dilwith put his face in his hands. "Why?" His eyes flooded and he blew his nose. "Why would Maeve do such a thing, Agent Hunter? She's always been so shy, quiet. Someone's feeding you a bunch of lies."

"Most likely for the money or the notoriety, Dr. Smoltz. I could show you the sites, but it seems sadistic to put your through that."

"You come in here with all this…this…I want to see the proof, Agent Hunter. Now!" He stood up. I followed him to his office where he motioned for me to sit at his computer. I found *Fearsome Ferry* site first, and hunted around until I found Maeve partying with three men. She seemed to be enjoying herself and completely alert.

"What did she do in the other videos, Agent Hunter? Tell me, please."

"Pretty much the same thing she's doing in the next site. She's on two different sites that I've found. There may be more."

"You mean her naked body went out all over the world on two porn sites?"

I looked up at his blood-shot eyes, glistening with tears. "I'm afraid so." I pulled up The Flash Van site and opened it at his insistence, rushing through thumbnails until Maeve appeared, using her real name. This one I hadn't even seen. I clicked to enlarge the picture and start the video. She hardly resembled Maeve, looking much younger than seventeen, with overly pink cheeks, a ribbon in her hair, and the red choker she'd had on when she died around her neck. Her thin, pale body stuffed with penises in every conceivable orifice. Dilwith began to sob as we heard a thud. Turning, we saw Tina Smoltz lying in a dead faint on the hall floor behind us.

I remembered a quote I'd once heard: "People cannot change truth, but truth can change people." I didn't know who'd said it, but it was profound. When I left the Smoltz house, I felt hollow for adding so much more pain to these parents whose lives were forever changed. I intended to scrub myself raw in a hot shower and try to get a good night's rest. Somehow I didn't think I could accomplish it.

8

I picked up my cell to dial Chase, but before I could, it vibrated.

"Hunter," I responded.

"Logan, it's Ken Poletti." My superior at headquarters had taken a more informal approach since the wedding.

"Good morning."

"Not so good. There's been another murder." He told me about an out-of-state student in Greenville—Tori Glenhouser—tossed into a Dumpster near East Carolina University. The message: yesterday's garbage.

"Even though this victim hasn't been a student at UNCW, I have to wonder if there's some link between Glenhouser and Maeve Smoltz. Agent McCracken is investigating in Greenville, but I've instructed him to compare notes with you. He'll be getting in touch. You guys need to figure this out. If they are related, work together to get the damn crud off the street. I'll warn you that McCracken can be a little bull-headed, but he's good and you can handle him." As usual, Poletti hung up without another word.

The murders could be coincidence. Tragedies happen, but my intuition slapped an ominous feeling around in my brain.

On the drive back to Genesis Beach I grabbed a meatball sub, some chips, and a drink, wanting to get back to the web site to see if Maeve or Tori were on it while I waited to hear from Agent McCracken.

~~~~~

The updated The Flash Van site offered some new pictures and a new letter that proudly boasted how easily the men picked up girls when told they'd get a thousand-dollar bill for agreeing to perform for a camera. They sometimes took girls to a ferry in an undisclosed location, according to the previous post I'd read.

I clicked on a video feed that showed a cute girl being offered money at a street café. She didn't look any older than fifteen, her long hair pulled back into dog-ears on each side with pink ribbons. Two men approached her with their backs to the camera. They had microphones pinned on. I could hear them offer her money for an hour of her time. She asked about the camera and they said they were filming everything for themselves and if she wanted the money she'd have to come with them. This cute but naïve girl only hesitated for a second, then grabbed her purse and left with total strangers. This scene horrified me.

The next video clip showed this same cute girl sitting on a couch in some dark place with the two disgusting men—I'd guess in their late fifties—one on each side of her. They appeared to be comfortable showing their faces on camera. The camera rolled, each man holding out a one-hundred-dollar bill and asking her to take off her blouse. She did it, and snatched the two bills and folded them in her palm. One man asked her to take off her bra for another hundred. She didn't hesitate. He gave her another hundred and the two men each sucked a breast.

The clip ended, and unsure I wanted to see anymore, I forced myself to continue. I didn't understand why she couldn't see where this behavior would lead. Or was she really that willing? She didn't appear to be drunk but alert and enjoying the attention and the money. I clicked the next video feed and she removed her shorts to reveal a tiny bikini with little pink rosebuds. The men were noticeably excited. They began running their hands all over her and inside the panties, exciting her as well. Her hands now clasped five one-hundred-dollar bills.

The next feed made me nauseous. She was completely naked, one man's penis inside her and the other man's thrusting down her throat. Neither of them wore condoms. I could barely see the money she held tightly in her fist.

I flipped the power switch. I couldn't take anymore and felt dirty for watching. She used the name Pansy and would be a thousand dollars richer. But what would it ultimately cost her?

9

I climbed the stairs between a silver blue Aston Martin coupe and a charcoal Ferrari convertible, both registered to Blaise Beaujue-Dufour. I wanted to know what Antonella knew about the pornographic web sites. When I knocked on the door, an older brunette snatched it open, her French accent strong and ugly. "Antonella, is this the woman who's harassing you?"

Antonella's face slid around the doorframe. She nodded.

"Investigating the murder of her roommate doesn't constitute harassment," I countered. "May I come in?" Antonella wrestled the door from the woman and opened it far enough for me to enter, flashing my badge at the woman.

"Agent Hunter, this is my mother, Blaise Beaujue-Dufour." I thrust my hand out but the woman didn't shake it. The level of hostility puzzled me. The gorgeous woman had to be in her forties although she didn't look it. Her hair pulled back in a ragged bun and her tanned skin glowed, making her angry steel-blue eyes pop. Her black dress, delicately fringed around the neck, framed a large chunky

Oriental necklace. Bronzed legs went on and on where the dress ended. The tapestry mules completed the look of perfection. She could be a model, but she must have flunked charm school.

"Ma'am, your daughter's roommate is dead. I'm trying to determine why. And there's been another murder, this time near the East Carolina campus. We're trying to find out if the two cases are related. Ms. Beaujue-Dufour, your daughter could be in danger."

The woman's eyes softened a bit. "Antonella, tell this woman what you know and maybe she'll stop coming around here. I have to go to work." She excused herself, leaving a chill in the air as she went.

"She's an interior decorator. She sells real estate too. I don't see her much," Antonella said. "Look, I'm sorry she was so rude to you. To be honest, I called her and told her I'd been questioned several times. She's just trying to protect me."

"And I could do my questioning downtown at the police station."

She fidgeted. "Agent Hunter, I'm not trying to be disrespectful. I just can't help you."

"You haven't tried." She looked down. "First of all, you and Maeve both have web cams. She was into porn. How about you?"

"No! My cam isn't hooked up, I swear! Look, I'll show you." She started toward her bedroom.

"You've had time to unplug it."

"No, please believe me." She let out a long, emphatic sigh. "Look, I came in one afternoon around three o'clock and Maeve was naked in front of her web cam, talking on the phone. I stared at her. She looked at me and grinned and never slowed down. Touching herself, purring into the phone. She didn't have the decency to close her door. I went right back out and drove away."

"Are you going to stand there and tell me you aren't into phone sex?"

Her hands trembled noticeably. "I've done a little, yeah. But phone sex only. No cams, no videos. Mama would kill me. You asked me why Rude approached me at Maeve's house? He tried to pressure me into using the cam, but I refused."

"I'm impressed," I added, "but you're involved with *Fearsome Ferry* and so is this Rude."

"No, not really."

"Not really?"

"Okay, I recruit some times, but that's it. I only go on it with recruits and drink and socialize a little, then leave before it sets sail. I've never even been in a private room."

"How do you manage to avoid that?" Antonella shrugged her shoulders and squirmed. "What about Rude?"

"He does some video. I really don't know much about that."

"Really?"

"Do I need a lawyer, Agent Hunter?"

"Not at the moment, but I'd advise you to have one on standby. This is an informal visit. If it becomes formal, it'll be downtown and you can call him from there." I slammed the door behind me for emphasis and heard her crying.

10

I slathered both sides of my banana sandwich with mayonnaise only stopping when the phone rang.

"Logan?"

"Chase?"

"Gosh, it's good to hear your voice," he responded.

"I miss you terribly," I croaked, not wanting to tear up.

"Yeah, I know. Me too. This is a ridiculous way to run a marriage."

"How's Fern, hon?"

"Not good. We're down to days, maybe hours."

"You want me to come?"

"When you can, but I know the case you're working on may prevent—"

"Not a chance in hell! I'll be there, Chase. I'm also calling Taryn and Pepper."

"Tell them I said 'hello', but I certainly don't expect them to rush up here."

"Taryn's only twenty miles from Asheville. She'd want to know. And Pepper will go if she can swing it."

I updated him on the two murder cases and what I'd uncovered on the Internet, and made plans to take leave and be by my husband's side, like he had been for me when my mother died.

~~~~~

By the time I cleared a short leave with Poletti, packed a few things, and drove to Asheville, Fern Railey had slipped into a coma. I sat with Chase on one side of her bed with Clive on the other, each of them holding a hand during her final moments.

"You know, she made all the funeral arrangements herself."

"Really? That's something, isn't it? You have to know it'll be what she really wanted." I poured the two men glasses of ice water.

Chase smiled at me. "Logan, one of the last things she said was how happy she was that I'd married you."

I smiled as Clive stood up, still holding Fern's hand. He leaned in.

"Chase, is she still breathing?"

Chase reached over to find a pulse with no success. A nurse tiptoed in and confirmed she had quietly slipped away from us forever.

~~~~~

Pepper and Taryn came to the funeral and sat with Chase, Clive, and me in the family section. The interior of The First Baptist Church of Asheville, built in 1927, was a gorgeous color of ivory and the enormous arrangements of flowers filled its front from wall to wall, every color in the rainbow displayed with many pops of pink. My favorite—the one Pepper sent—had huge sunflowers, cattails, and some kind of exotic bird feathers. Fern would have loved it. It was my first time inside the church even though I had admired its combination of Early Italian Renaissance and Art Deco exterior for years, its domed roof covered with graduated tiles of subtle colors, making it my favorite landmark in the city.

After the interment at Fern's family cemetery in Weaverville, Pepper headed back to Cary, and Chase and I followed Taryn up the mountain for a lavish lunch and a good romp with Homer. We wandered the valleys and fields around her property and spent the night, Chase not wanting to sleep in the big house he now owned in downtown Asheville. Taryn made certain we had everything we needed and promised a huge breakfast before heading to the other side of the big house so we could have privacy. I tried to comfort Chase as best I could, caressing him, kissing him, and letting him decide how to spend our night together.

"You know, Logan, she's always been such a sweet woman. You didn't get to know her all that well, but she was kind, generous—"

"I know, honey. A good mother."

"Yeah. She did her best under the circumstances." Chase referred to the difficult life she must have endured living with his father, a powerful attorney who succumbed to adultery and greed. We held hands in silence for a while before I spoke.

"I think Homer loves it here, don't you?"

"Oh yeah. He's one happy hound dog. Why wouldn't he love it? He can run until he's winded, chasing deer, bear, bobcats, wolves."

"Remember the wolf I saw when I lived with Taryn?"

"The one you got too close to?"

"Uh-huh," I giggled. "Not smart, I suppose, but he was so beautiful, and after the first encounter when he scared me in the fog, I wasn't afraid anymore for some reason."

"Well, like I said then, you're sometimes too trusting."

"Maybe so." I stirred beside him. "Chase, I know you've got time to decide, but we have the condo at Genesis Beach, the house in Asheville, and your cabin near Pisgah Forest. What are we going to do with all of it?"

"It's a lot to maintain, especially with us assigned all over the state at a moment's notice, but then again, they'd be nice to have for an assignment close to one of them."

"Maybe we should ask Poletti to assign us to the east coast or the mountains so we can use them all."

"Good luck with that one." As if on cue, my cell phone vibrated and I saw *SBI.gov* in the ID window.

Even though Poletti had given Chase the rest of the month off, he hadn't been able to do the same for me, calling at 10:30 p.m.

"Logan, before you drive back east, I want you to interview a couple not far from you," Poletti said.

"What's going on?"

"A girl from Polk County attended UNCW. She was murdered in Wilmington several years ago, but the case ran cold. I have a gut feeling she might be connected to the case you're working on." I didn't respond. "I want you to check it out." He gave me the names and address of the victim's parents, spoke to Chase for a few minutes, and ended the call.

We got quiet again, this time Chase moving closer and rubbing my shoulders.

"You're tense."

"I know, but I should be making you comfortable."

"I have the answer to that one." He pulled me into his arms for a tender, passionate, and emotional last night together for a while.

~~~~~

I screeched on top of the Hawsey Road exit and had to turn fast or risk going over an embankment, glad no traffic blocked my maneuver. A narrow road led me up and around for several miles. I pulled over on a wide shoulder to observe white smoke and abruptly watch it whisked away on the mountain breeze. A moonshine still? Maybe. My thoughts went back to my first SBI assignment—trying to sniff out bootleggers in these same mountains a little farther north. My efforts had been short-lived and futile as I lost myself in deep mountainous forests and hollows overrun with relentless kudzu, broke my glasses, and got my first skunking, all in the course of twenty-four hours.

I shook off the thoughts and pulled into the gravel road near a vineyard owned by the Tickle family. I had researched Belinda Tickle, the girl Poletti told me about, and learned she had been a freshman at UNCW four years earlier, had been badly beaten, raped, and left to die. She survived for a while in a vegetative state on life support. After about five months, her family made the decision to let her go. The case had never been solved.

A tiny woman met me at the door.

I flashed my badge. "Mrs. Tickle?"

"Agent Hunter, come in. We had a call to expect you, but I wasn't sure it would be today." She left the door open. The mountain breeze welcomed. "Have a seat."

"I think I'll stand for a few minutes if you don't mind. I've just driven from Asheville."

"Certainly. I understand." She turned slightly. "Paul! Paul! Come in here. The SBI's here."

I could hear Paul Tickle before I saw him: a wasted man, the clothes barely hanging on his frame. He shuffled his feet over to a dark red chair and eased into it as if it would hurt him.

Mrs. Tickle said, "He hasn't been the same since-"

"Irene, I hear you. Stop trying to whisper. You can't pull it off." She turned red and stared at the carpet. I sat down on a hard wooden bench, watching Irene Tickle hover over her husband.

"We know why you're here. Just get on with it," the man said, bitterness in his voice.

I cleared my throat. "Yes, sir." I opened my PDA to take notes.

"Are you taking pictures?"

"No, sir, this is just for recording." That seemed to satisfy him. "I'm sorry about your loss—"

"Woman, we're tired of hearing the sympathy. What I want to know is have you found this monster?" His eyes stabbed mine and I felt his pain.

"No, sir. I wish I could tell you he's in custody, but—"

"Custody? Hell! He needs to die!"

"Paul, please!"

"Hush, woman! Let me do the talking." Irene bit her lower lip.

"Mr. Tickle, I'm trying to find out if Belinda's death relates to a case I'm working on now. I need to ask some difficult questions. Hopefully, I can find your daughter's killer."

He nodded, eyes drawn back to the carpet.

"Did she have friends?"

"What kind of fool question is that? Of course she had friends. What are you trying to say?"

Difficult didn't seem to cover this conversation. "Sir, we can get this done quicker if you don't go on the defensive every time I say something."

"You women are all alike! Why didn't they send a man? A level-headed man?" He looked at the carpet again.

I stood up and glared at Mr. Paul Tickle, ready to go for the jugular. "I am level-headed. I have more balls than most men, sir, and I've had about enough of your disrespect. I'm here to try to solve the crime against your daughter, but you're such a damn chauvinist we're not getting anywhere, and we never will if you block every question I ask." I headed for the door.

"Wait!" he called out. I stopped as he motioned to his wife. "Irene, get us some tea." She quickly disappeared.

"Belinda was my flesh and bone, Agent Hunter. All these years have gone by and nothing's come of her murder, like we buried her and that's the end of it. It ain't right."

I walked over to him. "No, sir, it's not the end." I touched his arm as tears replaced bitterness in his eyes. "I'm bringing the killer to justice if there's any way possible, but I need to know more about her habits, likes, dislikes, who she hung around with, what she may have told you about college friends or even slight acquaintances. Any fears she may have had."

Irene came back with three glasses of divine sweet tea.

Mr. Tickle's eyes met mine. "Can we start this conversation over?"

"Yes, sir." I gulped a long swallow of refreshing iced tea and watched as they did the same.

"Okay, Agent Hunter." Paul Tickle shifted in his seat and writhed his way out of the big chair. "Let's go outside."

I followed him into the backyard and down a red clay and gravel road, walking slowly as he shuffled arthritic legs in silence. Irene followed far behind as if not certain she should come.

"You see them grape vines yonder?"

"Yes."

"My little girl and I planted them. Long rows at a time. For years. We've got over three thousand plants in six varieties. She loved to work out here. A real hands-on girl."

Mr. Tickle trudged to the end of a row of vines. "These here are Muscadine—American—and my personal favorite." He motioned toward more vines and ambled toward them.

"Over yonder is Barbara, an Italian grape, and back over yonder on that hill are the French varieties: Chardonnay, Cabernet Sauvignon, Merlot, and Viognier."

"Wow! This is impressive!"

"All of these do well in the Polk County soil. Some folks are raising Pinot Grigio and some others too. Did you know Polk County had the first cultivated grape vines in North Carolina?"

"No, sir, but that's interesting. I know you're proud of what Belinda accomplished."

"Was. Until that killer took her away from me...us. I don't mean to leave Irene out of this. She hurts too." We walked on and he pointed to a wild turkey on the ridge. "We have deer too."

"How about skunks?"

"Yep, all over these here mountains. You ever been skunked, Agent Hunter?"

"Yes, sir. Not a pleasant experience."

He attempted a weak laugh for the first time since my arrival. "Ask your questions." He abruptly stopped in his tracks. Irene sidled up beside him.

"Did Belinda like college?"

"Yep, enjoyed all of it. The studying too."

"What did she plan to major in?"

"Planned on a business degree. She wanted to come back here and turn this place into a winery." He looked down. "I thought it overly ambitious, but now there're vineyards sprouting up all over the mountains with their own little wineries, one a few miles from here. I guess she had the right idea all along."

"Why did a mountain girl go all the way to a college on the coast? Couldn't she get a business degree at Western Carolina, Appalachian, or UNC-Asheville?"

"Yes, but we didn't have much money for tuition, room and board, and books, so Irene's cousin who lives in

Wilmington, offered to let her move into a room at her house. All Belinda had to do was pay a little for groceries now and again."

"Did Belinda ever express any fears? Did she ever have a run-in with anybody?"

"Not that I know of." He turned to Irene. "You know of any?"

"No, she was a very confident, friendly girl, Agent Hunter. I think her only concern was not finding the money to get the winery off the ground. She struggled at two jobs to pay tuition. Like Paul said, we couldn't help her much." She got quiet when her husband glared at her.

"What kinds of jobs did she have?"

"Well, to be honest, she never really said much about one of them. She did have a waitress job, I know," Paul shuffled around. "Said most people didn't tip well."

"Yeah, she waited tables at some kind of tavern downtown. We didn't really approve, but she needed the job," Irene responded.

"Mrs. Tickle, do you know the name of this tavern?" She shook her head. I glanced at Mr. Tickle, who shook his head too.

"I believe it was a rowdy place; she mentioned that one time when she came home for a long weekend. Some of the customers made her uncomfortable," Irene said. Paul turned to face her. "You know, a pretty waitress in a bar is going to get hit on."

"How do you know that?" The man closed in on his wife's face.

"She told me so, Paul Tickle."

"Well, she never told me that."

We headed back toward the house. "Did she ever give you names? Can either of you think of any person she was close to? Anyone she might have been afraid of?

"Well, I…" Paul and I both looked at Irene. "There was this call from her a while before she was attacked."

"Go on."

"She was upset and said some man threatened her. I can't remember his last name, something strange. I'm not good with names. But his first name was Paul—that I can remember."

"Why did he threaten her?"

"She said he asked her out once and wanted her to do something illegal and she refused. I tol her to quit that job and find something else to do," Irene stated.

Paul was in her face again. "Why in tarnation didn't you tell me about it? I'd have gone there and beat the fire outta him!"

"Belinda made me promise not to tell you, Paul. She said she'd work it out." Irene's voice cracked, and she began to whimper. Paul didn't comfort her.

"Mrs. Tickle, did she say what illegal things he wanted her to do? I need for you to think carefully."

"No, she wouldn't ever say. She said she could handle it."

"Well, thank you for your cooperation. We'll try to find out where else she worked. Don't get your hopes up yet because this investigation is on-going. I'll be in touch when I have more questions or have anything I can share with you."

I left the Tickles and headed east across the state, leaving Chase behind to deal with the house, property, and heartache—happy Clive would be there to help with all the messy details.

11

Most of the UNCW dorms and apartments near the campus were empty now that summer had come, at least during the day. The only students around were taking summer classes. I cornered a dorm monitor and asked for home addresses for names on the list I'd gotten from the Smoltzes'.

Since Bailey Manley lived at Pelican Reach within the Wilmington city limits, I drove to the house in hopes of catching her there. The house looked new with a fresh landscape. I walked up the bricks to the front door, wide and stained, solid on the bottom and window-paned on top. Large white columns on the porch guided my eyes to a white rattan loveseat at the end. I'd noticed two white swings at opposite ends of the white balcony above the porch.

I rang the chime and waited for a response. The door opened. A stunning, light-complexioned lady guarded a smile. "Yes?"

"I'm Agent Logan Hunter, SBI. I need to speak with Bailey Manley, please."

"SBI?" Her eyes widened. "Come in, Agent Hunter. I'm Celyn Manley," the lady said with a sultry voice. "Bailey's my daughter. Come with me if you don't mind. I'm a caterer and getting ready to leave for a bridal tea."

"I don't want to inconvenience you, Ms. Manley. I apologize for not calling ahead."

"Oh, you're fine. I'm well organized, and I have an assistant who can load while we talk, but it'll have to be brief. I'm dressed, so at least I don't have to run upstairs and change." She had black straight hair pulled tight against her head and pinned in back. A wide metallic belt and necklace accentuated her understated black linen tank dress and tiny waist.

She led me through a great room I stopped to survey, overflowing with gorgeous bright colors and whimsy. Ms. Manley turned, "I'm also an artist. People are shocked at how unexpected the interior is, but I try to keep the exterior more in keeping with the rest of the neighborhood." The blue corner sofa framed a wicked metal table with a green top. An old dented car fender—license plate still intact—leaned against a long board, creating the most unusual mantle I'd ever seen. I felt certain the fender had a story to tell.

Sitting in the middle of the mantel, a large white rooster with striped fish on either side stared at me. A large wooden airplane stood on a stand against the white corner wall. Beside it, an appliquéd tapestry of children swinging. There didn't seem to be a theme for any of it, but nevertheless, it delighted me.

Celyn Manley's paintings continued into the dining room-turned art gallery, most abstract in brilliant colors. On some canvases I could recognize people or familiar articles; on others I couldn't. Ms. Manley walked me around the room and gave input when I seemed unsure.

"The figure is half-male, half-female."

Even though the figure and its body parts were brightly colored and infused into each other, I'd already determined it to be a human form. Other oil paintings were hands, some feet, others hands touching breasts, or hands holding feet, some more erotic than others.

"What do you think of these?"

"Intriguing."

She smiled and I followed her into the biggest and bluest kitchen I'd ever been in.

"Wow! The place is full of surprises. It's absolutely stunning, Ms. Manley." The wood floor, walls, and cabinets were painted ocean blue with a white table and chairs and countertops that kept the blue from overpowering. The stainless steel appliances looked great. The floor in front of the industrial-sized stove had well-worn paint.

"I stand there a lot; you can tell. I love cooking. It makes me so happy."

I could see why. Scones and other breads filled up the table, and she reached for a silicon mitt to extract some hot ones from the oven.

"Oh, Agent Hunter, will you go into that pantry and hand me the bowl of fruit?" The hot pink closet off the kitchen held shelves containing mixers, platters, crocks of spoons, whisks, and other kitchen gadgets along with spools holding a large array of aprons. Above the fruit bowl several odd bowls contained blooming pink flowers.

I scurried back to Ms. Manley. "I could stay here forever. No wonder you love it. It's a breath of fresh air."

"Thank you. Yes, it is, most of the time." She went to the door and called a man who came in and started transferring items to her Mercedes SUV. After he went out, she pushed the door closed.

"Agent Hunter, I'm concerned about Bailey. I've heard a few rumors here and there, but I can't find out what's going on. I'm afraid she's in trouble, but she clams up every time I try to talk with her. Your presence here indicates I'm right. She's in Cancun this week. I'd like to talk with you before she comes home, if that's possible, but not today."

"I'll be glad to come back or meet you somewhere."

"Has she done something wrong, Agent Hunter? I know you've questioned the French girl. Bailey didn't tell me; Antonella's mother did. That woman's upset with you, but I realize a girl is dead and you have to investigate. Antonella and the Smoltz girl were roommates, but I don't understand how Bailey could possibly be involved."

"Dr. and Mrs. Smoltz gave me a list of Maeve's friends and acquaintances. That's all, Ms. Manley. It's routine."

"I know she went to the poor girl's funeral, but I didn't really understand why. She just said she felt like she should go." So the wiry-haired girl in the embroidered sweater had been Bailey Manley.

We set a date to talk again, and I found my way back through the house, stopping one more time at several pieces of art before I let myself out.

12

As I drove past 300 Airlie Road with the Airlie Gardens entrance on my right, I eased over on the shoulder to take in the view. Sixty-seven acres of gardens by the sea included formal gardens, wildlife, walking trails, and fresh-water lakes. Azaleas and camellias bloomed yearly in spectacular glory, and it remained a favorite attraction during the Azalea Festival every year. I hadn't been into the gardens though, not since my childhood, and I didn't have time to ride through now.

On my left: The Cummings estate, where the next name on my list lived. I watched around a dozen thoroughbred horses running through the large pastures, swishing their tails as though they hadn't a care in the world, living better than many humans ever would. The Cummings estate and stables yelled wealth. So far the investigation had led me to many girls from affluent families, Maeve Smoltz coming from the most conservative on the list.

Holly Cummings hadn't attended the funeral but her name came up—an equestrian friend of Antonella's. I pulled into the long circular drive near the front of the house and saw her long straight hair bouncing as she rode a horse through the obstacle course in one of the fenced pastures. I rang the bell on the white stone house and turned away just as the large arched black door opened.

A graying man smiled and shoved his hand. "Agent Hunter?"

I nodded and flashed the badge.

"Do come in. I'm Nolan Cummings. Holly's exercising Storm Warning. She'll be up in a few minutes. In the meantime," he paused, letting me into the house, "my wife and I are here. Come on back."

I followed him into a tan living room with a dark hardwood floor and a stone fireplace, above it a large unframed picture of a majestic black quarter horse, possibly Storm Warning. The ceiling had trays with recessed lights. A lady with short silver hair I could see through rose with a bubbly smile of white teeth.

"Agent Hunter, please come in. I'm Noel, Holly's mother."

"I love the names."

"Both Christmas babies." Noel Cummings motioned me to a blue loveseat while she and her husband sat opposite me on the matching sofa.

"Dr. Cummings, I'm a little surprised to see you here since you're such a busy dentist."

"Yes, but when you called I readjusted a few patients to be here. I've been cutting back on my hours since Noel's cancer diagnosis anyway."

"I'm sorry. I didn't know."

"Oh, I'm doing so well he doesn't have to be here, but I certainly am enjoying his company and being spoiled. I'm going back to work at the Y soon."

"What do you do?"

"I'm a Pilates instructor. I miss it very much. The chemo pretty much took my energy, but I'm going in to do some light office work until I can take over classes again." Dr. Cummings kissed her forehead.

"Agent Hunter, Holly came home last weekend and emptied her soul, so to speak." He cleared his throat. "The three of us have been through so much, I guess her conscience got to her. We've tried to raise her right. Yes, she's spoiled, but she's never been a brat. She's very intelligent, and I don't, for the life of me, understand how she got herself into such a mess."

I tried to act like I knew what he was talking about.

Noel Cummings sat up and put her elbows on her knees. "She's a good girl, Agent Hunter. She searched for adventure—like most young people do—but she found evil instead. She's taking her time coming in. I hope you aren't too inconvenienced. We wanted to talk with you first. She's terribly ashamed of what's she's done but realizes it's time to come clean and get on with her life. I want you to get these sick bastards!"

"I think she got scared too, after Antonella's roommate died in such a horrible way," Nolan Cummings added.

Clearing my throat, I said, "I can tell you both that none of my SBI training prepared me for all I've uncovered so far during this investigation, and I don't think it's over by any means. Holly is doing the right thing to come clean and distance herself from all of it."

"So you think what Holly got into has something to do with the Smoltz girl's murder?"

"It's a possibility, but there are too many missing pieces to determine that at this time. Maybe Holly can help me fit a few of those pieces together." I cleared my throat again. "So how do you know Antonella?"

"We met Antonella and Blaise, her mother, at equestrian events. Holly and Antonella became instant friends although Antonella is much more extroverted."

The dentist stood. "Ladies, how about an early margarita?"

Noel clapped her hands and he pulled her to her feet, her rail-thin arms looking lost in the fuchsia tank top armholes. I stood and followed them to the kitchen with its cathedral ceiling. Dark mahogany cabinetry lined three of the walls and the same tan color as the living room made the space from their tops to the ceiling peak light and spacious. The floor, light gold terrazzo, matched the stove's backsplash. Red lilies stood enmasse in a tall clear vase on the sink island. I sipped, hearing Holly Cummings banging her shoes outside the glass doors.

A petite girl bounded into the kitchen, her long mousy brown hair now hanging lifeless. She resembled her father and had his oversized nose. Not a beauty, her smile revealed gleaming white teeth, no doubt, maintained by her father.

"Agent Hunter, I'm sorry to keep you waiting. Storm Warning wanted to be cantankerous." She held her hand out and I shook it.

"That's quite all right. I've enjoyed visiting with your parents."

"And that's our cue to get out of here. Pumpkin, we'll be upstairs if you need us. We'll be glad to sit in, if you want us to," Nolan Cummings offered.

"No, Dad. Take Mom up for a nap. I'm fine." Dr. and Mrs. Cummings shook my hand and disappeared.

"Oh, good!" Holly spotted another margarita. "Dad made me one. I guess he figured I needed it. Come on, Agent Hunter. Let's sit outside."

I followed her through the glass doors to a brick patio lined with colorful plants in full bloom. We sat at the umbrella table to nurse our drinks. A gorgeous cream-colored Persian rubbed my legs and I reached down to scrunch its fur.

"Agent Hunter—"

"Logan."

"Are you sure it's okay to call you Logan?"

I laughed. "Yep, that's my name."

"It seems too informal."

"I don't bestow that ticket on everyone. But your coming forward with key information in this investigation makes me feel I owe you that much. I know this is difficult for you."

"You have no idea." Holly Cummings inhaled her margarita, her skin flushed. "I really don't know where to begin. I must say I feel better since I spilled my guts to my folks. Even though I know it breaks their hearts, they're standing by me. I realize if we weren't close they'd have probably thrown me out and disowned me."

"You're fortunate to have such a great relationship. Many don't."

"Oh, I know that all too well. Antonella—you know, Antonella Beaujue-Dufour? She and her mother fight like two bitches in heat." Holly's hand flew over her mouth. "I'm sorry. I shouldn't have said that. It's just that they constantly argue. I can't bear to be around either of them anymore."

"What do they fight about?

"Everything—even boyfriends."

"I guess that's normal."

"No, you don't understand," Holly said, leaning in toward me. "They fight over the *same* boyfriends."

"You're kidding. I realize Antonella's mother is gorgeous, but—"

"Don't get me started on Blaise. She's not as reputable as you might think."

While I wanted to ask more about the Beaujue-Dufour, I figured I'd better let Holly get on with her own story before she changed her mind.

"Holly, you said you didn't know where to begin. Start at the beginning of this whole mess and tell me how you got to where you are now."

"I've had horses since I was about seven, but got serious about equestrian events in high school. I'd seen Antonella around but never really met her. She always had boys around her. I really think now some of them were more interested in Mommy—a real cougar. Anyway, we both went to UNCW here in town and ended up in a class together. We started talking about horses and over time became friends. I went to her apartment a few times and that's how I met Maeve Smoltz. She never had much to say to me, which, once I learned her awful reputation, didn't bother me at all.

"Antonella introduced me to Pete Crowder, who told me about a party boat and invited me to go with him one night. I thought it would be fun since I seldom dated, so about a week later, I went with him." Holly looked at the floor. "I should have known something was weird about it because it was so hard to get on the thing."

"What do you mean?"

"Well, he picked me up and started texting different people to find out the location of the boat. I asked him why it didn't dock at the waterfront downtown or somewhere like that, and he laughed and told me not everything about the party was legal. I figured he meant booze and drugs, you know? I shouldn't have gone, but I'm around that stuff all the time and just don't participate. He kept texting and calling around until he found out the boat's location."

"Are you talking about *Fearsome Ferry*?"

"Yeah, that's it. Sorry. I shouldn't have called it a boat, I guess. Anyway, he called it a private ferry and members called themselves a flash mob of sorts, and the people they invited to board and party were called sheeple. I thought it sounded kind of cute at the time. Some of them use Twitter and

Facebook to send one-liners about the location. All somebody has to do is follow a certain tweet and get the information. They use code words, I think."

I tried to file all this information. "Where did you and Pete board the ferry?"

"It was really pitch dark the night we went, but the ferry went up some creek off the Cape Fear River. We'd been through Landfall Drive already, with Pete knowing how to get past the guard like he was going to visit somebody. Then he said they—whoever they are—changed the location, and we had to go into Brunswick County to get there, I know that much. We drove down Old River Road, but then turned around. When we finally parked, Pete called the place Gator Creek. He looked at me like he'd made a terrible mistake by telling me that, laughed, and said he called it Sin Creek."

"Good name for it. And there's an Alligator Creek near there."

"That may be it."

"I'd imagine the sheeple have been told not to give out locations. He slipped up, which works for me," I said. Holly smiled and pulled the long hair out of her eyes.

"What happened once you got on the ferry?"

"We got on it and it moved away from the bank. I instantly knew I'd made a mistake. I saw Antonella wrapped up in friends, and Pete told me he would meet me back at his car later on that night. I asked him where he was going, and he said something about the second level." He just left me there. When I turned around, Antonella had disappeared too."

"Be glad he didn't take you to the second level. So is Antonella a member of this flash mob thing?"

"I guess so, or she could have been a sheeple like me. I really have no idea. You'd have to ask her. I'm no longer speaking to her."

"What happened then?"

"Some older guy handed me a drink and we started talking. He called himself a videographer. Stupid me, I asked him all about it, not realizing he actually worked on the ferry we were on. I'm naive, even more than I could ever imagine."

She sighed and looked off into the distance for a second.

"The ferry headed down Gator Creek and I got nauseated, so this older man said we could sit down in the room he used when he worked. Still nothing clicked with me. I think he put something in my drink because I got dizzy and the musty little room started to spin. I wore a pullover sweater and it soon came over my face. I tried to talk and pull my sweater back down, but I couldn't do anything. A horrible feeling—like in a house of mirrors at the fair. Everything out of focus, and all I could see were this guy's teeth, grinning at me." She wiped a tear. "It was awful, Agent Hunter."

"It sounds like GHB, Holly. About ten drops in a drink would put you in a dreamlike state, maybe semi-consciousness."

"The date rape drug?"

"Yep." I patted her hand. "I know this is really hard for you, but can you tell me any more?"

"I'm not sure what happened next, Agent Hunter, I swear to you." She looked toward the house. "I don't know if I passed out or if I just don't remember. I know I had sex. That much I know, but with whom I couldn't tell you."

"That's rape, Holly."

Her eyes flooded and her lips trembled. "I know."

"Could you identify this man, this videographer?"

"I doubt it."

"How about Pete?"

"Maybe, although I've been thinking about that and I remember how funny his hair looked. Like a wig, maybe.

The more I've thought about it, the more I think both men were wearing wigs."

"It would be smart to wear a disguise, I suppose, and maybe have a fake name too. Antonella probably knows him. I'd really like to rattle her cage." I had developed an ugly tone in my voice. "Holly, what you've told me so far is good information. I'm sorry to have to put you back through it, and I must warn you that when this all goes down, you'll be expected in court."

She nodded. "My parents already discussed that with me. There doesn't seem to be any way out of it."

"No, but at least you're alive and know to stay away from those people. I'm sure I can count on you not to give this investigation away."

"I won't tell a soul we've talked," Holly promised.

"Thanks. Now, getting back to Maeve, do you know if she ever went on the ferry?"

"The only thing I know is Maeve never had enough money, but when she went out, she'd overdo the makeup and dress like a little girl. She could pull it off too, you know? That innocent look. She and Antonella seemed like an odd couple to room together. Antonella didn't seem too happy with her. I don't know how they got together, but after Maeve died, Antonella acted different."

"How?"

"I don't know exactly. She got quieter, kind of withdrew a little, you know?"

"Like she felt guilty?"

"No! No, I'm not saying that. I don't know. It's hard to explain. Maybe it scared her. She just didn't call anymore. If I saw her, it was accidental."

"Did Antonella introduce Maeve to *Fearsome Ferry*?"

"I don't really know for sure. Maeve got into plenty of trouble without any help. I found out how wild she could be during spring break."

"Tell me about it," I said.

"Maeve flew with our group to Mazatlan in March."

I'd heard and seen plenty of televised shows about spring break, but never had the inclination to go fresh out of high school.

"Anyway, plenty of drinking and screwing around all the time. We'd rented an apartment near Capistrano, but we seldom saw each other. I stayed on the beach most of the time, getting this tan." She brushed her arm. "I did drink, but I didn't do the beer bongs, bombs, or chilly willys. You know, when you snort straight vodka." She paused for my response. I had none.

"One night tons of people came for a pill party in our apartment complex. Everybody poured whatever prescription drugs they had brought into a big bowl."

I'd heard of it. "Pharming."

"Yeah, with a twist. If you didn't contribute, you had to exchange sex for drugs. I had no intentions of contributing anything, so I left. I heard later that one of the guys who'd taken a lot of Viagra with some meth almost died. I saw some high school kids playing beer pong on the beach too. They were trashed. Some got locked up for vandalism and sexual assaults before daybreak.

"Now Maeve? She went wild. The boys chased after her the whole week 'cause they'd seen her on the Web. I heard they used Viagra so they could stay up all night. She was on something too. I know some kids use Red Bull and NoDoz to cram for exams and they do it to have sex all night too. I don't know for sure that's what she took, but Maeve had no emotional connection to people, Agent Hunter. She acted like a robotic rabbit. She just liked to screw, I guess. It didn't make any difference who, when, where, or how many times. She must have had sex a dozen times or more. When she finally surfaced late the next day, she looked like death warmed over." Her hands flew to her mouth. "Oh! I'm so sorry! I shouldn't have said that. I mean, since she's dead and all."

"It's okay. I just can't imagine anybody being that loose. It's astounding." We were both silent for a moment, and I wanted to change the subject away from Maeve. "Tell me who else from Wilmington went to Mazatlan."

"Let's see. Antonella, Tommy Trollinger, and the nasty geek everybody calls Rude. Bailey Manley chickened out at the last minute. I tried to tell her not everybody goes berserk, but she didn't want any part of it." Holly's head drooped. "She had the right idea. I'm sorry I went. Most people slept all day and were manic all night. Me? I was pretty miserable. I didn't fit in."

"I'm glad to know that about you."

"Yeah. I won't be going to spring break anymore. I'll go to one of our local beaches."

"Sounds like a good idea," I said. "Have you seen Bailey Manley on the ferry?"

"No, Bailey's basically Chicken Little. She apparently has more sense than I do, so I shouldn't call her names."

I offered no comment. "Were Tommy and Antonella a couple?"

"Not really. I only saw him twice and he and Rude filmed all the wild mess going on. Unbelievable, I tell you." Holly shook her head slowly. "I guess he intended to use the videos somehow. They didn't fly back with us either. Antonella said the guys only stayed about twenty-four hours."

13

I got directions at the Brunswick County Chamber of Commerce to Clover's Nursery and Landscaping, Inc. near Southport, drove down Jabbertown Road, and turned in at the rusty white metal gate entwined with various types of ivy. I continued down the blacktop, barely moving so I could enjoy the magnificent flowers and plants along the way. Blue and green hydrangeas filled most of the space between the drive and a wooden fence, which showed them off well. Wispy pampas grass waved from behind shorter plants. I smiled and pulled the Hummer around a curve where the drive became a cul-de-sac. Bold colors filled my eyes as I walked gravel paths in the direction of a building, barely visible in the distance.

I stepped around a huge bed of tiny flowers resembling a load of turned-over corn kernels. Shrubs were small and oriental, and ground covers crept beneath them and covered the ground until rocks, mulch, and stones put a halt to their wandering. I followed plush green grasses, seeing a little more of the building. I passed a Japanese-style garden and crossed a weathered footbridge surrounded on both sides by several types of ferns. Birds tweeted happily all around me. Who could blame them?

I stopped to drink in the delightful use of color in the next space, losing sight of the building again. I wandered around in a small circle until I heard voices and a curly-haired lady stepped into the path. "Good morning! Can we help you?" A Hispanic man stood behind her.

"I'm lost, but it's so beautiful in here I don't really mind it," I responded. "Are you Ms. Busic?"

"Clover, please. No one calls me Ms. Busic. Are you looking for anything in particular?"

"My name is Logan Hunter. I'm with the SBI, investigating the murder of a college student." Clover Busic turned to the man and said something in Spanish before he disappeared. The woman brushed her gloved hand through carroty curls and motioned me toward another path.

"SBI?"

I nodded.

"What on earth… Uh, let's talk at the house. Pedro can handle the pruning. I'm ready for some lemonade anyway. How about you?" She brushed trash off her blue-striped shirt.

"That sounds great." I let her lead the way, glancing back at me occasionally in silence. The two-story lilac house became more visible since the flower fields between it and us were daisies and other short plant varieties. Again colors mingled and the Queen Anne's Lace popped up in all its elegant whiteness here and there.

"Oh, tell me what this is called. It's gorgeous!" I reached out toward a flower, its throat embroidered with what appeared to be metallic thread.

"Salpiglossis. It's an annual and very few people ask for it. I don't think they're familiar with it. I may try to advertise it a little more. The gold is so unusual, and I love this particular color of vibrant violet." She smiled with obvious pride as she touched each one.

I could see the trellis on the white porch where extremely tall plants resided. We rounded the edge of the house and stepped on a tiled patio with a metal pergola. "Sit down, Agent Hunter, and I'll be right back with the lemonade." I made myself comfortable on a cement bench covered with an array of thick cushions for leaning back. Clover returned with a tray that held a pitcher of lemonade, glasses, and some square shortbread cookies. I enjoyed a couple of bites as the landscaper eyed me with suspicion. I jumped as a walking stick marched across the back of the cushion, no doubt heading for foliage.

"These are good. I seldom get homemade anything."

"I'll bet. Tell me, you said you're investigating a murder. I can't imagine how your investigation brought you here."

"Your daughter, Faith, actually."

"Faith? What do you mean?"

"Ms. Busic, her name's on a list the dead girl's parents gave us. I think her name was in the girl's cell phone book. I'm following up on each entry and questioning everyone mentioned to see if I can determine what really happened and why."

"But Faith? Who is this girl, this dead girl?"

"Maeve Smoltz, a freshman at the university."

"I remember seeing something about that in the newspaper. But Faith is a senior. I doubt she would even know any freshmen."

"Is she home, Ms. Busic?"

"No, not yet. She usually gets home around dark. She lived on campus but moved back home after her father moved out some months ago."

"I have to talk with her," I said again.

"Mama?" We both turned toward the house as Faith Busic headed our way. She had her mother's red hair in a darker shade and wore it long in softer ringlets.

"Faith, I didn't realize you were home. Come and meet Agent Hunter."

The girl stopped in her tracks and stared at me.

"Agent Hunter?"

I flashed my badge. "Hello, Faith. It's nice to meet you."

"What's this about?" She looked at her mother and back at me before Clover spoke.

"She needs to talk with you, Faith."

"Me? Why?"

"I'm investigating the murder of Maeve Smoltz and-"

"Wait! I had nothing to do with that! I don't know anything about it." She started to shake almost in a panic. "Really, Mama, I don't." She wasn't convincing.

"Faith, I understand you knew her," I added, drawing her attention back to me. "Your name is in her cell phone book."

"Really? Why would she list me? I barely knew her!" Her eyes darted back and forth between her mother and me.

"This is routine questioning. There's no need to be alarmed."

The Mexican man appeared and Clover whisked him away with an agitated arm and some strong Spanish that couldn't be cordial.

"Agent Hunter, I need to supervise Pedro. Can you come back later?"

"No, ma'am. I'd like to question Faith alone anyway. You go right ahead with your supervision."

"But," Clover glanced at her daughter, "do I need to get her a lawyer?"

"No, ma'am. As I said before, I'm here to ask a few questions. Nothing threatening."

Clover bobbed her head and reluctantly disappeared, but Faith stood still and quiet until I moved toward her.

"I want my mama here when you question me."

"That's fine, but you need to understand that you're an adult and my questions will be specific. I want details about your involvement with Maeve and the porn industry. If you have something to hide, maybe you'd better go ahead and call a lawyer. We can move this questioning downtown—"

"No!" Her pale skin flushed. "Oh God, I haven't..."

Faith looked around at all the shrubs and paths. "Let's go inside. I don't want Mama to hear this. She'd have a cow." I followed her through the kitchen door—which she promptly locked—and across a hardwood floor painted with diagonal black squares. We sat at the white table and Faith snatched a fresh pear from the large white bowl and offered me one.

"No thanks. Look, this is obviously difficult for you, but I need your cooperation. We can do this here or at the police—"

"No! No, please. Just give me a minute." She chomped nervously on the fruit, juice running down her beautiful scared face, her eyes darting left and right. I glanced around the kitchen and gave her time to compose herself. Three windows ran along a large white farm sink, and over the stainless-steel range cookbooks filled wood shelves to overflowing.

Faith sat up straight and locked her green eyes on me. "Agent Hunter, let's get this over with before Mama gets back."

"Tell me how you know Maeve."

"Maeve butted into every group she could. Freshmen boys weren't mature enough for her, she said. She showed up at a UNCW concert after-party and obviously some of the guys knew she was slutty. She left with two or three at first and then came back later for more. I had a few drinks and talked to friends. Of course, we talked about her because she was such a...well, you know, whore."

I said nothing.

"I sound cold-hearted, Agent Hunter, but I took an instant dislike to her. I'd never seen her before. I asked somebody who she was and found out her name. I didn't know her last name until the murder write-up came out in the *Wilmington Star News*.

"Is that the only time you were around her, Faith?"

"Unfortunately, no. She came up to me downtown one night after I'd had a few too many drinks. I'd just broken up with Scott, the boy I'd dated since high school. I intended to get drunk and was well on my way. She said there were a couple of guys who wanted to meet me, and she kinda pulled me along to Ann Street, I think it was. I remember some guys and a van. I've seen that van some since and it nauseates me every time I lay eyes on it.

"Anyway, I figured what the hell, I'd check these guys out, you know? As soon as we stepped into the van, it took off and headed over the bridge and down highway 421. The guys were kinda cute and asked me questions. Everything was cool for a few miles and then one guy whispered to Maeve and she stripped. Then all the guys dropped their pants and had a rainbow party with her."

"A rainbow party? What on earth is that?"

"Maeve dumped a bunch of lipsticks out of her purse and blew all the guys with different shades of lipstick. All the guys ended up with rainbow penises." I tried to envision that scene. "It's usually a lot of girls with wild colors of lipstick, but she did it all by herself.

"Then she slid up next to me and tried to kiss me. I pulled away. One of the guys said he'd give me one thousand dollars to have sex with Maeve while they filmed us. That sobered me up real fast. I pushed Maeve away and refused to cooperate with any of them. One guy tried to film but the older one told him to shut off the camera. That scared me a little bit because I didn't know what would happen next.

"Maeve and one of the guys suddenly jumped on each other and provided the cameraman with plenty to film. I was only inches from them. It was so disgusting! Then the driver slammed on brakes, threw the door open, and shoved me out in the dark."

"They left you on 421?"

"Yeah, way out where there were no businesses and no traffic at that time of night, somewhere around the Pender County line. My purse was on the van with my cell phone and everything else I had."

"What did you do?"

"I walked and cried for miles, scared they would come back and scared they wouldn't. I was afraid somebody even worse would try to pick me up. When I finally walked to a business, I saw a car and went to it, hoping somebody was there. A nice man rolled down the window, said he was just leaving work, and asked me what happened. He wanted to take me to the New Hanover County Sheriff's Office but I begged him not to, so he drove me to the beginning of Jabbertown Road and I walked on home. Mama wasn't home so I managed to get myself calmed down before the next morning. I called my friend, Holly, and we cried all night. She helped me cancel credit cards and all that shit the next day."

"That would be Holly Cummings, I presume."

"Yeah."

"So you already know Holly's been on the ferry?"

"Yeah, but Agent Hunter, we're not bad girls. We really aren't. It's just—I don't know—we want to have some fun— the right kind of fun, of course—but it's hard to trust anybody anymore."

"I understand, but you need to tell your mother about this. When it all comes out, we'll need your testimony to put these perverts away. Don't let her find out from somebody else."

I left a distraught Faith Busic at the table and worked my way back to the Hummer without running into her mother again.

14

Trying to get to Cameron Mekkelsen's house in the country reminded me of the drive to Chase's cabin in the remote Blue Ridge Mountains, only the terrain was more or less flat here rather than roller-coaster hilly. Limbs and branches reaching out to squeak on the sides of the Hummer framed the road.

I'd found Cameron on *Fearsome Ferry* web site and recognized the college senior with the long flowing, thick blonde mane as UNCW's Homecoming Queen. Beautiful, flawless skin, big doe eyes, major in textiles. Had she gone looking for *Fearsome Ferry* or had the ferry's unsavory barnacles reached out to her?

I learned that once the video showed up on the Internet, she packed her bags and headed home. I wanted to know if fear or just embarrassment sent her packing. The dirt road turned into gravel in front of two brick columns that framed an open old wood gate. I drove through, and the cabin—if you wanted to call it that—came into view. Not the small rustic cabin I'd expected. Instead a large two-story gray farmhouse with dark orange doors and trim greeted me.

I got out and started the long walk up uneven pavers, taking in the bounty of beautiful foliage and brilliant blooms on both sides. Not paying close attention, I nearly ate cement. I caught myself on my forearms, saving my face but scraping the skin on both of them. I hopped up and looked back at the culprit: a paver two to four inches askew, lying in wait for an SBI agent enjoying the yard on the way to interrogate the occupants of the house.

The orange door opened and a broad smile spread across the lady's face.

"Ms. Mekkelsen?"

"Yes? You startled me." Her bottled blonde hair and complexion resembled Cameron. "Can I help you?"

"I'm sorry to come unannounced, Ms. Mekkelsen, but I'm trying to locate your daughter, Cameron." I presented my badge. "I'm Agent Hunter."

"Oh dear, whatever would you need Cameron for?" She stared for a second. "Oh, my manners. Please come in. I came out to get the mail." She scooped a letter from the box on the side of the house.

"Is she here, Ms. Mekkelsen?"

"Marie, Marie Mekkelsen. Agent Hunter, what's going on?"

"Perhaps you've read about the freshman, Maeve Smoltz who was recently murdered."

"Yes, but what's that got to do with Cameron?"

"Ms. Mekkelsen, I really need to talk with her." I put a little edge in my voice to move things along. I had spent far too much time with defensive parents instead of the girls I needed to interview.

"I sent her to the Piggly-Wiggly, but she should be back any second."

"Would you mind if I wash my hands? I tripped on the way up your walk." I showed her my scrapes.

"I'm so sorry! I've been trying to get someone out here to fix it. I love the stones, but they sometimes shift and become uneven. Let me show you to the bathroom. By the way, don't be shocked. I collect antique mirrors, among other things. You'll see yourself from every angle."

She wasn't kidding about a room full of mirrors. Grooved ledges of various lengths surrounded the four walls, with mirrors of every shape and size leaning on them. Small ones hung on the wall with ribbon framing one with twelve tiny round mirrors inside it. Some mirrors were tarnished, but the arrangement worked. I washed my hands and the scrapes and returned to the black-striped chair she sat in.

"I love the mirrors, and your quilts are so beautiful. Did you do them yourself?"

"Some, and Cameron has done a few, but mostly I buy them at antique stores. Come on back. I'll show you a few goodies while we're waiting for Cameron. And I don't mean to pry. I'm concerned about her, Agent Hunter. She moved home recently. She said she didn't feel safe since the murder. I must admit I'm glad to have her home though."

We walked into a room with quilts on every wall, setting off an old white church pew, a white dining table with a gold mirror, and a battered tray table. A large sign that read *Grocery and Crockery* hung above it. My eyes caught sight of the two-toned green stove from great grandma's day, covered with old pots and pans, cooking utensils, and antique linens.

I followed Marie Mekkelsen into the modern kitchen, feeling like I'd left one century and entered another at the doorframe. The floor and cabinets were dark wood. Down lights highlighted special items in the room. My eyes drank it all in as I heard the back door open and turned to meet the eyes of Cameron Mekkelsen.

Marie Mekkelsen greeted her daughter, one of the prettiest girls I'd interviewed in this case. I felt certain the men of *Fearsome Ferry* loved the long mane of blonde hair that fell over both shoulders and ended below her breasts.

"Cameron, this is Agent Hunter with the SBI. She needs to talk to you for some reason."

Cameron's eyes shot through me.

"Why? I mean, SBI? Gosh, what in the world?" Cameron flopped into a kitchen chair. I sat across from her. Her mother stood, not knowing what to do.

"Cameron, I have a few routine questions concerning Maeve Smoltz. I understand you knew her." I turned to her mother. "I'll let Cameron decide whether we do this privately or with you here." I looked first at Marie and then at Cameron, whose eyes reddened and watered while her face blanched.

"How much do you know, Agent Hunter, and how much is speculation?" Cameron reached for a tissue.

"I know a great deal. I know some very specific things about you, Cameron."

She looked down as her mother went to her. "For Heaven's sake, I'm sure Cameron hasn't done anything illegal, Agent Hunter."

"Mama, listen to me. I have to talk to her. I don't think I can stand to have you here while I do. Please excuse us. And don't eavesdrop. I'll tell you later, I promise. There's no point in keeping any more secrets, is there, Agent Hunter?"

"No, Cameron. It's all coming out in the open. Everyone you know will soon know. Your mother has a right to be told first."

Marie grabbed two hands full of her own hair. "Oh, God! You two are driving me to the looney bin!"

"Look, Mama, please don't make this any more difficult than it is." Her mother stared at her, kissed her forehead, and went out the back door, mumbling and shaking her wavy hair.

"I know this is terribly hard for you, Cameron, but we have to do this. You seem far too mature to have been mixed up in pornography."

"Apparently I'm not as mature or smart as I thought." She cleared her throat. "Where do I begin?"

"Start at the beginning. How did you get involved in *Fearsome Ferry*?"

"Oh, God! Have you been on the web site?"

"Along with millions of other people around the world, Cameron—some sexual predators, some perverts—looking for a beautiful girl like you. It's a billion-dollar industry." She lowered her head and blushed crimson. "Surely you knew that would happen."

"No, no, I had no idea, Agent Hunter! I took some elective classes and met this guy, Tommy Trollinger. I dated him a few times. He was always a gentleman to me, really. He never pushed for sex, but treated me like a lady. Then he dropped out of school. He said his business had become so big he didn't need the degree. He never told me what business though.

"Then I had a class with Faith Busic. Have you met her?"

I nodded.

"Well, she introduced me to Holly Cummings, who knew Antonella, the girl from France. We'd sit at tables during break and they'd talk about the van and the ferry. When I asked questions, Antonella invited me to go to *Fearsome Ferry* one night. I guess I'm naïve for my age. I didn't know how rough and ugly it could get. Faith and Holly didn't go with us.

"Stupid me, I went, and since I'd had a sucky week, I drank far too much. Everybody there drank a lot. Everything went fine until, at some point—very late—two guys came over and started talking to us. We laughed and giggled. I recognized Tommy, but these people called him "Tit", because his name is Thomas Irving Trollinger. He owned this business. Whispering started and girls started pairing off with guys. After Antonella left the table, Tommy said his pal, Rude, wanted to dance with me. He was nasty-looking, but I got up to dance. I figured, what the heck, you know? It was just a dance. I kinda stumbled, and Tommy said I could stretch out in his office if I'd had too much to drink. I trusted him for some strange reason.

"Agent Hunter, I've never gotten myself into that kind of situation before. I'm twenty-one, for Heaven's sake. But the booze controlled me at that point, I guess. I told him I wanted to leave and he laughed. He said we were a long way from shore; was I a good swimmer? I guess I started getting seasick and didn't know it. I let Tommy and Rude help me to the room. But it wasn't an office, more like a mini studio. I backed up but Tommy stood in front of the door, told me how beautiful I looked and how I could make a quick thousand just by taking off my clothes and letting him film me. Nothing else. He promised there'd be no sex.

"I figured I'd get out of the room faster if I undressed and got it over with. I thought I could trust Tommy, you know? I wasn't thinking straight, that's for sure."

"What happened then, Cameron?"

They handed me another drink and I downed it, thinking it was the same as I'd been drinking. Boy, was I wrong! I got really hot, sweaty, and kinda in a daze. This Rude started pulling my clothes off. I protested, but I didn't have the strength to stop him. I tried to scream out but all I heard was my own pitiful whimpering."

"It sounds like the date-rape drug. They may be using it to make things a whole lot easier. Some other girls I've interviewed had a similar experience."

"God! I hadn't thought about being drugged." She patted her forehead. "After my clothes were off, I felt so weak I sat down in an over-sized chair. Rude stood close by but he didn't touch me. Tommy had turned on the camera and told me to spread my legs around the front edges of the chair and to lean back and arch my back so my breasts would stick out more."

Tears filled her eyes, and she stood up and went to the sink. She kept her back to me and continued. "I don't know how long he filmed. I'm not sure if I passed out, or what. I don't remember any more. The next thing I can really recall is stumbling off *Fearsome Ferry*, fully dressed, with some other girls. Most of them were laughing and showing off their money. I puked my guts out."

"Do you think Antonella set you up?"

"No, not really. But some of the girls I saw actually enjoyed themselves, Agent Hunter. Can you believe that? They said they liked the money, and I think the danger made it exciting to them. I don't know if they got the same treatment I did, but I couldn't look at myself in the mirror when I got to my apartment. A couple of days later I heard Maeve Smoltz died a horrible death, and she'd been one of the girls going to the ferry and to a van called The Flash Van.

"Antonella said Tommy asked about me; he wanted to see me again. I told her I was through with the whole sordid affair. She said 'You're not gonna tell on us, are you?' like a five-year-old. I got to thinking about all of it and called my mother to tell her I wanted to move back home."

"Are you afraid of Tommy or any of the others?"

"Maybe, I don't know. I just wanted out of it. I hope I never see any of them again. I was scared I'd run into some of them on campus. I don't socialize much at all now. I'm so glad I've graduated."

"I think those two guys hook up with girls off campus or on the Web. Have you seen the site, Cameron?"

She nodded, sobbing now.

"I can tell you that Tommy flunked out. He had horrible grades his freshman year and the dean put him on academic probation. He had to attend summer school to register for fall classes. He didn't."

"Instead, he launched a career in graduate-level sleaze."

"Yeah."

"You did the right thing by getting out. It may have saved your life. I appreciate your cooperation, Cameron. The SBI is determined to bring down this operation. I'll get out of here for now, but I may have more questions later." I handed her my card. "Please let me know if anyone tries to contact you. And don't meet with Tommy at any time."

"You don't have to worry about that, Agent Hunter."

"I'll see myself out."

"Now comes the hardest part of all," Cameron almost whispered.

"What's that?"

"Breaking my mother's heart."

15

Pepper called me with the surprising news that she had met a Wilmington businessman and started dating again. She apparently spent the night with him in the port city and wanted to meet me for dinner somewhere. I told her The Union Café overlooking The Cape Fear Riverwalk would be good for me, so we made a date to meet at the wood-planked walk on the waterfront near dusk. I circled the downtown cobblestone streets several times before finding a space big enough for the Hummer near the horse-drawn carriage rides that transported tourists through the historic district from Water Street to Second Street by Market Street. The carriages were replicas of nineteenth century French evening coaches that moved behind the horse at about four miles per hour. Wilmington boasted over three hundred blocks of historic homes, including The Bellamy Mansion. I fed a meter for three hours, got a polite tip of a top hat from a carriage driver, and turned the corner, looking up at many church spires on my way.

Pepper, dressed in a gauzy turquoise tank over white pants, hugged me tight and long.

"Gosh, it's good to see you! Logan, you're stunning. Love the tan. Life is good, huh?" Pepper's grin revealed pristine teeth.

"It's good." The tan came from being outside most of the time, but it only covered my face and arms. My legs were ghostly white, but I didn't confess.

"And how's hunky Chase?"

"He's still handling Fern's estate. It seems she had endless stocks, bonds, and property," I replied.

"I'm sure it's a sad time for him. I remember almost going crazy trying to sort out Rick's stuff. It helped that I had a good lawyer to lend a hand with it." I remembered what a rough time Pepper had when Rick Teater was murdered at Genesis Beach. He had been planning to propose to her and I found the five-carat diamond ring during my investigation. He had already made her beneficiary of his entire estate without her knowledge.

"Yes, he has Clive there to help and a trusted family attorney too." I shifted. "Now, without further delay, I want to know who your new man is, where you met him, all the details." We ordered lobster bisque and salad, pulling our chairs closer.

"It's been kind of a whirlwind romance, Logan. I hope I'm doing the right thing," Pepper started. "I met him about a year ago but only because of our mutual restaurants. We were both at a food show, had a couple of drinks, and went our separate ways. Then he came to the restaurant to eat one night, and I recognized him. He stayed until we closed, and then we stayed up all night talking. It's like I'd known him forever. I felt comfortable, you know?"

"Pepper, I'm thrilled that you're finally moving on."

"I know I've held on to the past long enough."

I had to agree. Even though Rick Teater had left her his fortune—including the Hummer she'd given me—the times had been difficult for her. But she pulled herself together and opened Pepper's, the restaurant she had dreamed of but previously couldn't afford.

"So what's this lucky man's name?"

"His name is Saul, Saul Turrentine."

I listened to my friend's plans to visit the port city often over the coming months. This pleased me since I'd get to see more of her as long as my current case kept me here or near my condo at Genesis Beach.

I glanced behind her at a noisy party coming in, among them the good-looking young man from Maeve's funeral, who walked by with two young ladies and sat across the room from us. He wore a black baseball cap with white lettering: The Man, The Myth, The Legend.

Could this guy be Tit?

I kept looking over at him and hoped he didn't recognize me. Handsome enough to be a model, he had flawless skin, dark eyes, and thick lashes. He had a delicate mouth— enough to be female—but he was definitely male and the ladies had his undivided attention. I turned my chair with more of my back to him, but I could see his reflection in the French door's glass.

"Logan? Are you listening?"

"Yeah, sure."

Our food arrived and we ate like we hadn't had a bite of food in several days, the conversation little short blurts of congeniality and giggles. Once we finished, Pepper started to get up. I put my hand across the table for her to sit down. "Wait just a minute. I need more water." The waiter filled my glass as the threesome across the room walked out.

"Let's go, Pepper." I stood up as they went around the corner.

"But you wanted more water."

"I changed my mind," I smiled, pulling on her arm. Once we were outside, Pepper snatched her arm back.

"Okay, what's going on? You haven't listened to one word I said."

"I'm sorry, but that guy is somehow involved in a case I'm investigating. I need to follow him."

"I'm going with you."

"No, it could be dangerous."

"Logan, I didn't call you to be ignored," Pepper snapped. Reluctantly I tugged her arm and we ran across the cobblestones to the river's edge. I heard the lady at the depot say, "Good evening, Mr. Trollinger."

I watched as the threesome boarded a large ferry, barely visible in the night fog. As the ferry turned to follow the flow of the Cape Fear River, I managed to see the name written in bold red letters on its side: *Fearsome Ferry*.

"Well, I'll be damned."

"What? What is it, Logan?"

"I can't explain it right now, Pepper, but this is a big break in my case." We headed for the depot and approached the ticket master.

"We don't sell tickets to board that particular ferry, ma'am. You have to be a private member. You need a specific ID pass. I'm sorry, you're not allowed." The ticket master, a security guard, and a good one at that, wouldn't budge, but I hadn't completely struck out. I'd learned something of significant importance: Tommy "Tit" Trollinger and *Fearsome Ferry* were connected. That was all the valuable information I would get on this trip. I had put the face with the name and malicious reputation.

I could now give Pepper my attention for the rest of the time we had left.

"Logan, I want you to be my attendant," she blurted out.

"You're marrying this guy?"

"That's what I've been trying to tell you, you ninny!" She asked me to be her only attendant in a small ceremony in the garden she'd finished beside her one-of-a-kind restaurant in Cary. I heard myself tell her I would, barring any unforeseen SBI assignment. I'm sure the shock showed on my face. Who was this man? Wasn't she rushing things a bit?

"It's okay, Logan. I'm a big girl. I know it seems sudden, but like I said, I met him over a year ago, and we're so comfortable with each other."

"But, Pepper, what do you really know about this guy?"

"Give me some credit, will you?" I wanted a better response but didn't get it.

We entered a tavern on Dock Street and headed for the bar, barely able to see or make our way through the musty-smelling crowd—mostly men. As we perched on our stools, I realized the waiters all wore black leather thongs and open leather vests. I didn't get down to their feet before I realized we'd made a terrible mistake. Dick didn't own the bar on Dock Street. The sign over the mirror read: Dicks on Dock, not Dick's on Dock.

"Pepper, this place is a stinking armpit!" I hollered at her through deafening music.

"I think it's a gay bar, Logan," Pepper shouted back at me.

"You think?"

"Just relax."

I glared at her. "And we're here because?"

"Well, I didn't realize it until we got in the door, but since we're here, let's see what these guys do. You know, check it out. It's not like they're going to pick us up or anything."

She had a point. "But Pepper—" A leather-covered penis rubbed my elbow. "Hey!"

"Sorry. It's crowded in here." I looked up at the tall waiter, black hair, hard tanned bare chest, his eyes boring holes in me as though he were on a mission.

"Keep that thing contained," I said, pointing as his crotch-cutter wiggled like a caged animal about to break free. He winked. I wanted to neuter the smile spreading over his face as well as the one at his crotch. He hurried away as if reading my mind.

I grabbed Pepper's arm. "He's not gay!"

"Yeah, he is."

"No, hell no, he isn't!"

"He's here, isn't he?" We both watched the man's tight butt disappear around the corner of the bar. "Now that's a damn shame," Pepper added.

"I'm telling you that man is straight. Rubbing up to me aroused him," I said, putting my hand on her wrist for emphasis.

"Maybe he's here to experiment, Logan. He could already have been aroused by another man before he got over here to you."

"Humor me, will you? Let's go. I'm uncomfortable in here." Pepper pouted as we held hands and worked our way to the tavern door.

~~~~~

When Pepper drove away, I put more money in the meter and walked back to the dock where I hoped *Fearsome Ferry* would return to let passengers off. It didn't.

After miserable hours near the river's steamy air, I headed back to the Hummer with intentions of getting a good night's sleep at Genesis Beach. I yanked a blue business card from under the wiper, tired of being subjected to advertising gimmicks stuck there. I crammed it in my pocket and headed for the condo.

I thought about Pepper on the ride home. She'd mentioned her new man, in his sixties, while she had just turned forty. I hoped she hadn't found some old crotchety man looking for a sugar tit to sweeten old age. Pepper had been hurt enough.

On the way out of town on Highway 17, I rode by a large seafood restaurant named Turrentine's. The outside suffered from neglect even though apparently open for business. I wanted to be happy for Pepper, but something about it bugged me. Maybe the surprise of not only Pepper's return to dating, but that she already planned to marry the man. Maybe once I met him, I'd see the magic and relax a bit.

~~~~~

I locked up for the night and fished the blue card from my pocket: "Call me. We need to talk." No name. Just a phone number. I usually ignored such messages, but I dialed the number and it went straight to voicemail. "This is McCracken. Leave a message."

So this was the agent joining me on the murder case. He hadn't taken a course in telephone manners, that's for sure, and while I'd never met him, his deep voice sounded somehow familiar. He evidently knew what I drove and had been downtown tonight as well.

"This is Agent Hunter. I'm assuming you left a card under my wiper." I hung up, having nothing further to say. I could play Bad Ass too.

~~~~~

I went to O-yes-ter's, another riverfront bar, late the next afternoon and carried my binoculars. I dressed in tight clothes, showing off my long can-tanned legs, and what little cleavage I had, to fit in with the young folks downtown this time of day who were dressed to kill, or at least, to solicit. I was in the hunt, wanting to figure a way to get on

Fearsome Ferry without putting myself in a compromising position. Tommy "Tit" Trollinger had seen me before, and some of the girls had probably told him about me. I stayed near the depot, but the ferry never came in.

Heat overtaking me, I stopped for a strawberry daiquiri ice cream cone at The Leaky Tiki. "Well, I guess I missed the boat," I said to the bartender, a large redhead. "Do you know when it comes back in?"

She eyed me with suspicion. "It seems to have a strange schedule. Doesn't dock here much. Only when there's something big going on that pulls the law away. All I know is you have to be escorted on by a member; otherwise, you don't get on. Were you meeting someone?"

"Not really. I heard I could meet some guys on it."

"Yeah, you can do that for sure."

"Have you ever been on the ferry?"

"Nope. Don't plan to neither. I'm happy making drinks and minding my own business. That'll be seven-fifty."

I paid and sipped. I saw her talking to a man at the end of the bar, who smiled at me when I looked that way. I smiled too. The bartender walked back over.

"You may be able to get on The Flash Van, if you're interested."

"What's that?"

"I heard the same people who own the ferry own the van, but it stays on the streets. They pick you up, you pose for some pictures, and they drop you off and pay you for your time—an hour, max."

"Surely there's got to be more to it than that. Who are they? And what kind of pictures?"

"You sure you're not a cop? You ask a lot of questions, and you don't look like the kind who'd want to go for a ride."

"I might be if I knew what you were really talking about. You're so vague."

She glanced at the man at the end of the bar. "I can't really say. Just heard gossip, really. Don't know much about it." She looked at the man again and shut down that particular conversation, so I tried another approach.

"Do you know a girl named Belinda Tickle?" I asked her.

"Tickle? Yeah, I remember that name. Hard not to. She used to work here a few years ago. Sweet girl. From the mountains, if I remember correctly."

"Yeah. She told me about the ferry thing."

"I guess she went home. I don't really know. We have so many college kids who work while they're in school and then head out. Some only stay a semester. Lots of turnover here."

"Did she work somewhere else too? I'm thinking she actually had two jobs."

She glanced at the end of the bar. "Uh, I wouldn't know." Her hands started to shake as she ducked them under the bar. I glanced at the man at the other end, who looked away as I stared at him.

I decided not to tell her Belinda Tickle was dead, but see if I could get more information or at least deduce if the man intimidated her.

"I've heard that ferry docks somewhere up Gator Creek, but I'm not sure where."

"Oh, it moves around constantly, I hear. Sometimes it's around Eagle Island or Keg Island. Goes down the Brunswick River too." She flushed when she saw the man staring at her from the other end of the counter and leaned toward me. "I can't really say anything else. Enjoy your drink."

She walked away and didn't come back. Bingo! She was afraid to talk. The question: why?

16

I walked out on the only pier at Snow's Cut Park, some
distance from where a catamaran pulled into the marsh
off River Road, and gazed at the water teasing its few lights.
It was peaceful and quiet here, but I felt an evil undertow
pulling those curious enough into water too deep to escape,
into decadence from which they might never surface.

Mesmerized, I watched a white crane standing in the
marsh scoop up an unsuspecting fish. It shook its meal down
and crept around the edge of the water before lowering its
head in false repose—a piece of rigid statuary—biding its
time for a second helping.

The day's blowtorch heat had stolen much of my energy,
but I swatted at the whine of mosquitoes who wanted a
meal as the sun lowered over the waterway, turning the
horizon into swirls of strawberry juice. I smiled in spite of
my grumpy mood.

After a few trance-like minutes, I heard steps behind
me and turned with caution, watching a well-dressed man
as he staggered down the pier toward me, not battling
drunkenness but a stiff wind that had erupted, blowing head-

on. I had to wrap my arms around myself and hug the railing to keep from toppling over the weathered boards myself.

I continued to keep my eyes on the man as he walked to the other side of the pier and held onto the rail with one hand while he pulled his coat collar up around his ears, saying nothing. This didn't feel right. I sensed danger. My cell phone rang and I answered with relief. It was Chase. The time had come for me to head back to shore.

"Your timing is perfect," I said aloud, scurrying toward land.

"Hey, hon," Chase crooned.

"Chase, I'm in a high wind. Hold on until I get to the Hummer. I can't hear you."

The man gave me the heebie-jeebies. I couldn't see his face, I didn't know his intentions, but something knotted my stomach. He looked oddly familiar, but it was hard to tell with him wrapped up like a mummy. I walked off the pier, pretending to look at the water from time to time, really glancing back to make sure he didn't come up behind me.

Once I got into the Hummer I locked the door, feeling vulnerable for some reason. I saw another note on the windshield. Where the hell had this one come from? There was nobody else around but the man on the pier. My connection with Chase had been severed. I dialed while I kept my eyes on the pier.

"Okay, Chase, I'm back. Miss me?"

"Unbelievably." He sounded in pain. "I can't seem to get back to you. Sorry you married me?"

"Never! What's going on to keep you from coming to Wilmington?"

"I finished up the estate paperwork, and Clive agreed to stay on and keep the house running."

"I thought Clive wanted to go back to England."

"He's undecided, so he'll stay put for a while and re-evaluate things later. I think he's lost without Mother. And it'll give us time to decide what to do with all of our estates."

"I guess so."

"Yeah. Anyway, my news is bad. My first day back on the job, we have another dead college girl. I thought you'd want to know right away. The ME ruled it mechanical asphyxia."

"Isn't that—"

"When somebody sits on the chest or back and the victim can't breathe."

"Murder?"

"I'm not sure if this case will be considered homicide or accident. The coroner said she'd been engaging in some mighty rough sex."

"Are there any links to porn?"

"Yeah. A witness said she'd been picked up by a van called The Flash Van, did whatever the men wanted, and they dropped her off somewhere. My understanding is she'd done this more than once, knowing they filmed it and put it online."

"Chase, did you say The Flash Van? Where?"

"Boone."

"Wait a minute, there's more than one van with that name?"

"Yep, maybe there's a fleet of them. This could be just the tip of the iceberg, Logan. We'd better check university towns around the state, maybe all over the country. I wish we had more manpower on this." He sighed. "By the way, I understand Farris McCracken's been assigned to the case. He likes to do undercover work. Guess you'll be seeing him in Wilmington."

"I found a card on my windshield to call him, but I haven't met him yet."

"Watch out around him, Logan. Other agents say he's moody and difficult to work with. Major ego and a lady's man, I hear. He tries to get into all the panties he can."

"What has that got to do with me? I'm married."

"Just warning you. I don't trust this guy."

"I can handle myself."

"I know. I didn't mean to imply otherwise. Old Crack better watch himself, huh?"

"Crack?"

"His nickname."

Chase gave me an idea of when he might be back on the coast and I blew him kisses through the phone and got out long enough to snatch the note off the windshield wiper and get back inside. The neon pink paper had three words on it: *Suck, Bang, Blow*.

Was the man on the pier some pervert sending me a sexual invitation? I drove to a gas station to fill up the Hummer, putting most of the one-hundred-dollar bill in the tank while my hands shook. I slid back inside and buckled up for the last leg home, locked up, and grabbed a cold Smirnoff's Mango cooler while the web site loaded.

Viewing got more revolting as I went through videos and thumbnails. The first page loaded twin lesbians with dildos, the second, a man clipping clothespins on a woman's nipples and clit, but the third one was more than I could bear: a woman who appeared to be retarded, being raped right on my computer screen by a big bulk of a man whose face wasn't visible. The violence made me race to the bathroom to throw up.

Honk! Honk! Honk!

Grabbing my Glock, I opened the door, eased out and around the bushes and sides of the condo, and headed toward the Hummer. Something had set off its alarm. As I went around the back of it, I stared into the frightened eyes of a young Hispanic girl sitting on the grass.

"Don't shoot! Please to help me," she pleaded in a heavy Spanish accent. I walked toward her and told her to stay seated and put her hands on her head. She did, trembling.

"Who are you? Where did you come from?"

"I climb in when you stop for gas. Please, don't to shoot me. I had to get away from them." She had nothing in her hands. No purse, no nothing. I told her to stand up when she started to cry. She wobbled up. I grabbed her arm and helped her to the house, looking around in every direction to avoid being ambushed.

Once inside, she sat down on the foyer floor and crossed her legs Indian-style. I stared at her for a minute, maybe longer.

"Who are you running from? Wait a minute. Who are you?"

"Skarleth. Skarleth Menendez." She was probably pretty underneath all the filth and stink. I'm surprised I hadn't smelled her in the back of the Hummer.

I sat down on the floor away from her. "How old are you?"

"Fourteen."

"Do you live around here?"

"Where am I?"

"You're at Genesis Beach. You got in the Hummer between here and Wilmington, the port city."

"What state is this?"

"State? You don't know what state you're in?" She shook her head. "Oh, You're in North Carolina."

"Carolina? I'm from Mexico. I not know where my family is. We got apart coming over."

I had already figured out that she was in the United States illegally. "How long ago?"

"I not know."

She cried while I decided what to do. If I called authorities, they'd take her away to God only knew where. If I didn't make the call, I had to help her, somehow.

"You look hungry." She nodded. "Let's get some food in you." We stood up and I headed for the kitchen with her following me. She wobbled again. "Are you hurt?"

"Something wrong…down there." She pointed to her privates.

I wondered if she'd been raped. I'd planned to feed her and then let her bathe while I found her some clothes to put on. If she'd been raped, we needed to go to the hospital before she had a bath.

"Did somebody rape you?"

She whimpered. "Many times."

"Oh, my God! We need to go to the hospital. Here, eat this apple and these chips on the way."

She grabbed my arm. "No, Miss."

"Skarleth, we need to get rape evidence and you need to identify who did this to you. I'm with the SBI and I'll personally find the bastard. I promise."

"Bastards, Miss. Many, over a long time. Miss, I can't describe any of them. There have been mucho. Mucho! I don't want to remember!"

"Okay. Okay, I'm fixing you something substantial to eat and then you're getting a bubble bath while I pull out some clothes. You're about my size, only much shorter. I can find something to fit you even if we have to roll up sleeves."

Skarleth smiled for the first time. "You not arrest me?"

"Arrest you? No, I want to help you if I can, but you've got to be honest with me." She nodded and devoured the apple and a bag of chips. I didn't have much to cook but bacon and eggs, which she inhaled as though her life depended on them.

I laid out a towel and cloth, some shampoo, and started a tub of Coconut Lime Bubble Bath. "Soak as long as you like. I'll put some clothes on the bed for you. Here's some shampoo. I'll be downstairs."

"Thanks."

I found some shorts that would hit Skarleth about capri-length, a tank, and underwear. I didn't know if she could wear one of my bras since she happened to be more endowed at fourteen than I was at thirty. I gathered her filthy clothes with gloves on and discovered she wore no bra anyway.

Once I disposed of the offensive clothes, I headed for my computer. This time I wanted to read every word for clues to the location of the main headquarters or the Webmaster. I found mention of Appalachian State University and East Carolina University in tiny print. Apparently The Flash Van ran between these universities and UNCW, possibly UNC-Asheville too, or there were multiple vans across the state picking up college girls; I'd seen one in Wilmington almost daily. Someone edited videos and broadcast them around the world, a lucrative, disgusting business that, no doubt, had made its founders filthy rich.

I typed in *www.suckbangblow.com*. The monitor filled with bright balloons, party hats, cups and straws, and all types of party supplies and toys, nothing pornographic. I had to admit they'd picked an attention-getting name for their store. I put the note in my files in case it somehow connected to the investigation. I still wondered how the note got on my windshield at Snow's Cut Park.

"Uh hum."

I turned to see a girl I didn't recognize, dressed in my clothes. "Wow! You clean up nice," I said as a grin spread across her pretty face.

"I thank you so much for your clothes and the wonderful bath. I'm puckered. I hated to get out, so I stayed until the water was too cold."

"I'm glad you enjoyed it, Skarleth." I whirled around in my chair and leaned toward her. "Sit. Tell me how you got into such a mess."

She began to tell me the sad story of the past two years, her father having sold her into prostitution in order to get himself into the United States illegally. Her mother had also been sold. Somewhere along the way, they'd been separated. She had no idea what became of her mother. "I can only hope she found someone as kind as you, Miss."

I hadn't told her my name. "I'm Logan."

"Logan. That's a pretty name. You said you are SBI. What is that?"

"I investigate crimes. I'm working on a big case now that involves many girls about your age. They're involved in the porn industry. In fact, a van and a ferry operate in Wilmington."

Skarleth hung her head. "Yes, I know of it. I think this ferry is a boat, no?"

"Yes. How do you know that?"

"The men they take me on a big boat somewhere on a river, I think. But some man on the boat he got angry and said I had disease, and they threw me and the men who took me there off the boat. He said I'd infect his customers."

"Did you see the name of the boat? Did it have several levels? Describe the man."

My barrage of questions confused her. "Very handsome, but not nice. Like I said, he mad with the men who took me there. He threw us all off. I think the boat bigger than most, but not like a cruise ship or anything. I didn't see a name."

I whirled around to the computer and typed in *Fearsome Ferry* site. "Come here, Skarleth. See if this looks familiar."

The screen filled with naked girls and a tiny picture of the ferry in the top left corner.

"Yes, like that."

"Describe this man. You said he was nice-looking. What else?"

"He had dark, thick hair. Dressed nice. Very neat and clean, not like the men who took me."

He sounded like Tit.

Skarleth suddenly doubled over.

"What's wrong?"

"I hurt, in my stomach. I have sores." I picked up the phone and called the beach medical clinic a few blocks from my house. I loaded Skarleth into the Hummer and drove her over for a physical.

Dr. Hope Jenys examined Skarleth and spoke to me while the young girl dressed. "She has both gonorrhea and chlamydia. I'm putting her on some strong antibiotics, Logan. I also tested for HIV. I'll let you know."

"Hope, what should I do? I can't keep her. My job takes me all over the state."

"I'll call somebody. They can help her find an Hispanic foster family and get the medical treatment she needs. She also needs to be in school."

Relieved, I told Skarleth about the foster care and she seemed okay with it. Dr. Jenys gave her some medicines and instructions before she came back to me.

"Miss Logan, thank you for caring. I'm not going home with you. Dr. Jenys has somebody to pick me up from here."

"Good luck, honey."

She hugged me and I left her, hoping she'd be placed with a good family. On the way home I stopped and bought a gallon of Clorox to disinfect my bathtub. While leaving her bothered me, I knew it had been the right thing to do.

17

I'll have Wham Bam Shrimp and a lettuce wedge drizzled with the Chef's Special Dressing. Can I add a loaded potato to that order?"

The waiter nodded, setting down the white Zinfandel I'd already ordered. I sipped, realizing my hunger for the first time. Few people were downtown anywhere, which surprised me since Memorial Day usually brought out more tourists. I guessed they'd gone to the nearby beaches instead. I'd decided to have lunch and stay put on the Finz terrace to observe any activity on the streets below that might help move the stalled investigation forward. I didn't know what else to do. I had binoculars but needed to be as discreet as possible.

I enjoyed the shrimp and lettuce even though the dressing failed to live up to my expectations. I played around with the potato, eating only the middle and pushing the rest around on my plate. The waiter appeared with another glass of white Z.

"I didn't order this."

"The gentleman over there sent it by way of introduction." I followed his hand into the enclosed room I'd walked through to get to my table until it stopped at a tanned, buff, good-looking man, wearing a Conk's tee shirt that read: Pack my Meat. He sidled over before I could refuse the drink. I felt anger rising.

He slid his long jeaned body into the chair opposite mine.

"I didn't accept this drink."

"You will."

What an arrogant prick!

"Will not!"

"Will too," he retorted, thrusting a napkin in my direction.

"Listen—"

"Look under the napkin, but don't give me away." My gaze met his as I hesitantly lifted the paper corner, expecting to see a condom, but instead staring at an SBI badge like my own.

"You're—"

"McCracken, but I'll let you call me Crack."

"Is that wise crack or ass crack?"

He made a half-snicker. "Not interested in having a pissing contest with you right now, Hunter. We need to talk, but not here."

I remembered Chase's warning. This man exuded mega doses of testosterone. "I'm not going anywhere with you. Hey, wait a minute!" I pointed at him. "You're the jerk who bumped me in the gay bar, wearing little more than a smile."

He grinned with unabated conceit. "Memorable for you, was it?"

"Actually, I didn't appreciate your privates rubbing my arm."

"Most women don't seem to mind my Evinrude rubbing them."

"I'm not most women, and this conversation is over!" I slid to the edge of the table before his long arm clamped over my wrist.

"Hear me out. We're both working on the same…" he glanced around "uh, project. We need to go somewhere with not so many eyes and ears and compare notes." I hesitated. "I'll try to behave myself. Meet me at the crotch of the tree."

I left first, and bad ass SBI Agent McCracken came along a few minutes later. We individually crossed the street to the park on the Cape Fear riverfront, more or less private except for an occasional passerby heading toward the Hilton Riverfront Hotel. I found the tree, obvious because the trunk separated into two large sections, forming a sizable upside down crotch.

"Okay, spit it out, McCracken."

He walked away from me, turned, and crouched, staring at me and saying nothing.

"What is this?" I screamed it.

"Keep your tits in your bra," he almost whispered, looking around. "Just making sure we're alone."

I glanced around. "Do you think you were followed?"

He laughed. "Not a chance."

"So?"

"Maybe you were."

"I'm careful."

"Good girl." I wanted to wallop him. "Okay, I know you're working the Smoltz case. I got Glenhouser."

"Yeah, my husband told me."

"Railey your husband?" I nodded. "Lucky bastard." His voice changed and he actually grew a decent smile.

"He's not a bastard."

"Sorry. Poor choice of words." He pulled out two pieces of Bazooka bubblegum and tossed me one. "I don't share with just anyone."

"So I suppose this is your way of bonding."

Time passed as we sized each other up, neither willing to say much until we were comfortable enough, as if I could ever feel comfortable with this man. I couldn't help but notice his open fly. I tried to ignore it, but after a moment, I simply couldn't help myself.

"Your pony is leaving the stable."

He glanced down and yanked up the zipper. "Pony? I'll have you know there's a Clydesdale in these britches."

I laughed—loud. He turned red, not from embarrassment but more than likely anger.

"We need to join forces," he uttered through clinched white teeth.

"I'd rather eat concrete."

"Why so hostile, Hunter? Still hung up on my johnson?"

I gulped and felt the heat rise in my cheeks. Yep, I suppose I could be hung up on that. I stared into the distance and then at him, his electric eyes immediately withering my stare. I looked at the ground where most of my composure lay in a heap.

"We both might be eating concrete before this case is over. We got drugs, we got booze, we got phenomenal raunch, more than even *I* can tolerate. I need to know what you've found out and fill you in on what I've learned so far," McCracken said.

"Porn sites, *Fearsome Ferry*, the van. I suppose you know all that?"

"I know about the sites, but I'm not good at computers. Somebody else'll have to dig deep to find out the source behind that stuff. I don't know anything about a van. But I'm planning to get on that ferry one way or another." He paused. "I may have to be a bad boy, but, hey, it's a sacrifice I'm willing to make for the common good." His face closed in on mine.

"It's common, all right."

My remark caused him to guffaw.

"You know, Hunter, I could get used to you."

"I don't share the same sentiment."

He cocked his head, apparently amused. "We're playing with a rough crowd. I haven't figured out who's behind all this stuff, but you can bet your sweet ass they'll do whatever they can to stop us from taking them down. We need to be on the same wavelength."

I knew that but didn't admit it, ready to move the conversation forward.

"You investigated the Glenhouser murder."

"Yeah. Tori—an ECU freshman from Cleveland, Ohio—black, barely five feet tall, weighing less than one hundred pounds. Her mother said she planned to come to Wilmington and audition as an extra on *One Tree Hill*. You know, lots of kids think they can get on television or into a movie out at the Screen Gems Studio. She never got the chance." I knew that the film studio had a great reputation and attracted young and old alike, and that hundreds of films and television episodes had been filmed in and around the port city, sometimes called "Hollywood East".

"Tori's mother flew in to Greenville to throw around what little weight she had. She threatened to sue the university and told cops and me she wanted immediate action. Not a pleasant lady. No witnesses to the murder as far as we know right now. The coroner thinks she died some time before she got thrown in the Dumpster, but we don't know where or exactly when. Mrs. Glenhouser had no idea who Tori's friends were, or if she even had any."

"Why was Tori at East Carolina rather than somewhere in Ohio? That might give us a clue."

"I asked Mrs. Glenhouser that very question. She said Tori left Ohio to get away from her parents who argued all the time and finally separated after she left. She only went home once during the entire semester and then only for three days. She never mentioned any friends, but she was majoring in music and played several musical instruments. Mommy suggested I try the university's music department. I did. They barely knew the girl, said she seldom showed up for class and never practiced."

"Sounds like she might have been involved in something more interesting than class," I said.

"That wouldn't be all that difficult."

One issue that linked Maeve to Tori—their parents had no clue about who they hung around with or what they did in their spare time. Giving them freedom was admirable and necessary, but being clueless was irresponsible.

Something caught my eye across the river. I fished out my Bushnells, zeroing in on someone on the deck of *Fearsome Ferry*, now docked across the river in Brunswick County, on the same side as the *USS North Carolina* battleship. I ran to a tree at the river's edge.

"Hey! Wait up," McCracken called out and soon slid up beside me. "What you got?"

"Hang on a sec," I said.

Tit, the dark-haired handsome man undoubtedly involved in the porn ferry and perhaps the vans and the web sites, moved around the deck, waiting for someone.

"*Fearsome Ferry*. Blatantly docked right over there. That's Thomas Irving Trollinger on deck, looking considerably stressed out."

He nudged my elbow. "Let me see."

"Where are your nocs?"

"Uh, run over by a city bus last week. Come on, Hunter, let me see the guy."

I passed him my binoculars and he took them with a degree of embarrassment.

"So do we think he's a player?"

"Tit is a major player."

"Tit?"

"Initials for Thomas Irving Trollinger. That's what the young ladies I've talked with call him."

"Cute. Kind of fits his lifestyle, doesn't it?" He grinned at me. I snatched the Bushnells back and refocused on the ferry's deck.

"He's got company."

The nasty guy, Rude, who'd approached Antonella at the Smoltz home, walked up and boarded when Trollinger let down a small metal boarding ramp. Then Trollinger shoved Rude as they engaged in an obvious disagreement. I wished I were in earshot. Tit pointed a finger and got in Rude's face before disappearing inside the ferry, followed by the puke face, waving his arms in frustration.

"We need to get on that ferry while it's docked," McCracken said.

"We'd have to drive over the bridge and take 421 to Old River Road over in Brunswick County to get close to it," I figured. "Interesting that it seems to be hidden in broad daylight."

"Yeah. All the cops are over at the Bellamy Mansion where Vice President Biden is supposed to come in later today. Big event. The Secret Service has been here for two days and police and deputies are involved. Probably some of our guys as well. There's no telling what'll go on in this town while they're tied up over there." He paused. "Hey, we could take a small boat across to the ferry."

"We'd be sitting ducks."

"For once I think you're right, Hunter," he said, nodding.

"For once?" I nipped hot air. "What the hell does that mean, you asshole?"

"Geez! Why so sensitive? I'm just playing with you. You gotta get used to me."

"Yeah, I'm sensitive about Poletti sending a condescending—"

McCracken threw up his hands. "I shouldn't have said that. I don't know you well enough to say that. I have a unique sense of humor, that's all."

"Get the hell away from me!"

"Look, I'm sorry, okay?"

"I'm going to work. Without you. We don't need to stay together. We'll compare notes occasionally, and that's as far as it goes."

"That does kinda make sense. I'm a loner. I do my best work undercover any way. You stay public. Maybe we can both figure a way to get on the ferry."

"We?"

"Don't you think we both need to get on there?"

"I suppose." But I wasn't really looking forward to boarding the *S.S. Sleaze*, with or without the wise crack. We separated after promising to answer each other's calls and texts to stay in touch.

I walked down the brick street and crossed over to the depot used by various boats, ferries, and barges, now closed and chained. I walked to the corner news stand and picked up a local magazine so I could continue to keep an eye on things as more folks moved into the harbor area. Bon Jovi's picture appeared on the cover, the big celeb in town over at Trask Coliseum on the UNCW campus. No wonder law-enforcement supervisors assigned every available officer to work either the vice president's event or the UNCW event. I wondered if anyone would show up down on the riverfront until after the concert. I'd read the magazine from cover to cover by the time the harbor bustled with activity, wishing I'd had front row Bon Jovi tickets myself.

A lady appeared and opened the depot. I watched as *Fearsome Ferry* slowly left the other side of the river and headed in my direction. What audacity! How blatant could they get? But I hadn't seen a single cop since I'd been here today, not one. The owners of the ferry were certainly in the know and bold enough to take the opportunity to pull right up to The Riverwalk.

Young women, dressed in everything from low-ride jeans, halter-tops, and sandals to cocktail dresses and four-inch heels appeared from side streets and cabs. They went to the depot, showed a pass, and boarded *Fearsome Ferry*. Most laughed and seemed excited about boarding. One looked my way, close to tears. So why do this? Nobody pointed a gun at her.

After the crowd of men and women boarded and disappeared into rooms on the ferry, I again approached the depot lady.

"Excuse me."

"Oh, I remember you. Look, if you want to get on, you have to have a working pass or be the guest of a member."

"How would I get to be a member?"

Her posture stiffened. "I can't help you with that. Please step aside now." Several men walked up behind me, all appearing to be fine upstanding professionals, about to board the porn ferry. Three looked like attorneys. One looked me over and winked. I walked over to the harbor stairs and sat down, observing and still within earshot.

"Good evening, Mr. Turrentine," the depot lady said sweetly.

My head flew up.

Pepper's fiancé? No way! I couldn't get a good look at his face, but the name fit.

He whispered to the woman who apologized for using his real name. He nodded, and boarded.

"Pardon me again, ma'am. That's Mr. Turrentine? Saul Turrentine?"

The depot woman, no longer friendly, said, "You need to go home. Stop asking so many questions. You're going to get yourself and me in trouble. I told you this is a private party boat. Now go away before I report you to the owner!"

"And who might that be?"

Her arm shot out with a pointed finger, gesturing me to go away. It took all my strength not to yank out my badge and proceed around her. But if I created a scene, I'd be vulnerable and lose any leads I'd gathered. I needed to be discreet and maintain my anonymity long enough to put deep gashes in *Fearsome Ferry's* hull.

I looked around as a man in a business suit cleared his throat, being escorted on the boat by a pretty lady. He winked at me. McCracken? Damn it! How had he changed clothes and managed to get on the ferry while I stood here unable to do the same?

Damn, he's good.

18

Tired of hanging out down New Hanover County's desolate River Road and getting nowhere, I called Chase, still investigating the ASU murder case in Boone.

"I've done about all I can do here, so I'm heading east soon. By the way, this girl went to Wilmington right much. Seems she often visited a cousin of hers down there, so we may be able to make a connection between her and the other victims. As for any porn charges, if these people are all consenting adults, we may end up with egg all over our asses."

"But they're not, Chase. They can't be. Some of the girls look under eighteen to me. The web site is full of under-aged girls they're filming either here or on the vans. I found a horrible rape online, filmed in a house somewhere."

"There don't seem to be any limits to how low these bastards will stoop to get what they want. We'll get them, Logan. Just rest up for a day or two and don't move on the ferry or van until I can get there to help."

I remained quiet.

"Logan? You hear me? Don't do anything that could put you in danger. They'll continue to run the operation, so there's no hurry."

I had the right to remain silent.

"Logan, are you listening?"

~~~~~

The next afternoon I tried to reach Pepper to set a lunch date for some time that week. I tried to take Chase's advice as I swung in my hammock in a wonderful breeze on the condo's deck and dialed, my mind still on Mr. Turrentine. I needed to let her know what I'd learned about her fiancé. If he got his rocks off on *Fearsome Ferry*, why did he need to marry her? For the money she inherited from her lover? Most likely. Her heart had been broken when Rick Teater died, and now she'd fallen for a perverted jerk. I had to stop her from marrying this creep.

"I'd like to speak to Pepper Ellis, please. This is Logan Hunter calling," I told the sous chef at Pepper's.

"Hi, Agent Hunter. I'm sorry, Chef Ellis has taken a few days off. She's getting married, you know. She's in Wilmington with her fiancé."

She's still nearby! I twisted out of the hammock, found my sandals, and headed for the door, dialing her cell number. I got voicemail.

"Pepper, this is Logan. Call me immediately! It's urgent!"

It would take me close to an hour to get to Wilmington and then I didn't know where she and her pervert fiancé might be. Would he take her down to the harbor or would he take her somewhere private, maybe to his own house? I had no idea where to start. I hoped she'd check her voicemail soon.

I didn't slow down to change clothes, wearing short shorts and tank, no makeup and sandals that weren't good for running if a situation arose. I needed a plan. I couldn't find Pepper and expect her to walk out with me. She'd want an explanation, and Saul Turrentine would probably put up a fight. I needed to think, come up with a strategy to get her away from this leach.

I drove to the harbor since I had no idea where else to start. I didn't even know what kind of vehicle he drove. I parked and fed the meter, pushing the .22 caliber—the only weapon I had with me—deeper into my shorts pocket.

I dialed her cell again. Still no answer. I resigned myself to waiting for her to call me back. Even though not in official attire and equipment, I headed to the boat ramp near the group home. The time had come to do a little surveillance around that house. My gut told me so.

I stood near the huge Cape Fear Memorial Bridge and looked at the boat landing through my binoculars, turning slowly toward the green three-story house on the other side of a vacant lot. I didn't see anyone outside, but knew retarded adults—mostly women—lived in it. I watched an old man fishing in the Cape Fear, but his luck was like mine, fishless. I walked into the vacant lot to get a better look at the house without being extremely conspicuous. I could always swing my nocs back toward the river if someone appeared.

Venus flytraps thrived in the sandy soil beneath my feet. I maneuvered around them. I'd read in *The Wilmington Star News* that the rare plants only grow within a sixty-mile radius and only in this Cape Fear region. I had one as a child, fascinated at watching it catch and consume an unsuspecting fly. I also learned that the Cape Fear River reverses course when the Atlantic Ocean approaches high tide—a significant tidbit for riverboat and ferry schedules. And I found out Alligator Creek dead ends. That meant the ferry must turn around and come back out or be stranded and become an easy target for law enforcement foaming at the mouth to catch it.

One of the witnesses I questioned told me the ferry had boarded passengers at this boat landing at least one time, so I scanned the pavement and grassy area between it and the group home's property. If they'd been here, they left no trace.

My phone vibrated. "Hunter."

"Where have you been, Hunter?" McCracken sounded angry.

"What's it to you?"

"Get off it, will you? We need to talk."

"Go ahead."

"I'm on Old River Road in Brunswick County. I just left Southport. It seems our little ferry gets around."

"What do you mean?"

"That floating sex machine has plenty of private docks all up and down the lower Cape Fear, down the ICW, and even near Fort Fisher and Bald Head Island."

"Bald Head?" Bald Head Island is located off the coast of Southport and accessible only by private boat or a passenger ferry. What knowledge I had about the island was sparse, but I assumed the wealthy electric-car-driving residents had chosen that island to avoid everything that wasn't ritzy and first-class.

"I saw people being transported from the marina to the ferry by catamarans with my own eyes."

"Catamarans? Geez! I've seen a catamaran in the marsh near Snow's Cut Park. They've got it planned well, haven't they?"

"I suppose if the water is too shallow for the ferry to come in, they set up the catamaran service. And it keeps prying eyes like mine too far away to do much about it. They're in and out too fast to catch."

"Interesting to know."

"Oh, by the way, Hunter, after I ate at Eb & Flo's Steam Bar, I picked up a loaf of freshly baked bread at The Maritime Market."

My stomach gnawed at the mention of fresh bread. "And you're telling me this because?"

"Well, I planned to share with you, but you're such a snit I'm not sure I will."

A snit? Well, maybe a little.

"When Railey gets here, you two ought to head over to Bald Head for the sand sculpting. It's awesome what these artists are sculpting out of sand and water." I'd like nothing better than to take time off to recreate at Bald Head, but I didn't see that happening.

"Gator Creek is only one of many places the ferry docks long enough to collect clients and then moves on. It stays out most of the night, and let me tell you, what goes on is unbelievable," McCracken said.

"Yeah, I couldn't help but notice you were on it."

"Got lucky."

I wasn't biting on that one, no siree.

"Hunter? You still there?"

"Yep."

"I overheard a conversation on there. About law enforcement. Don't know if there's any truth to it, but it sounded like the ferry covers water in Brunswick, New Hanover, and possibly Pender Counties. Supposedly The Coast Guard Marine Patrol has jurisdiction in the ocean, ICW, and up to the mouth of the river. Then The Cape Fear River Police have authority down to the mouth. The way the ferry moves around keeps the law confused and uncooperative. Nobody's sure who has jurisdiction on a given night."

"That's a smart move by the bad guys. And about The Coast Guard…"

"Yeah?"

"Don't they have a berth downtown at The Riverwalk? Why haven't they gotten involved in trying to stop *Fearsome Ferry?*"

"Well, in case you haven't noticed, the one guard ship that docks there is at sea."

"Oh."

"That's a good question, though, because it does moor down there across from the battleship. Somebody told me once that it's actually a working ship and stays at sea at least half the year. With the new alerts on terrorism, that may well be their top priority."

"I guess that makes sense. But McCracken, since that ferry is moving up and down the Cape Fear River, it goes right by Sunny Point. I'm surprised that the ferry hasn't been inspected by the Army."

"Good observation. I'm sure they have plenty of security around that ammo depot. Could be the ferry passes that area with great caution."

"Yeah, good strategy," I said. "While the county officers and city police try to figure out who's in charge, the ferry glides on down the river and up and down the waterway. I guess that's where the flash mobs and sheeple create enough confusion to keep the boat afloat, so to speak."

"Sheeple? You're losing me again."

Advantage Hunter. "I've been told that someone behind the scenes concocted communication on cell phones and computers for clients, called 'sheeple' because they follow directions and find the ferry since it moves around so much. 'Flash mob' is what they call the group once they converge on the ferry, or wherever they're supposed to meet up. They're sworn to secrecy, I guess, to keep people like us from figuring it out. I found out by interviewing some kids who've been on it and had an unpleasant experience."

"Any possibility of a rogue cop or deputy on the take too?"

"Without a doubt. Money talks. That makes it easier to hide."

"I suppose. Oh, by the way, Chase will be here soon. We can cover more ground and water with him on board."

"Great." His voice didn't sound appreciative.

My cell beeped.

"Gotta go. Got an incoming call." I closed my phone without a gracious departure.

"Logan? Logan! It's Pepper. You called and said it was urgent. What on earth is wrong?"

"Oh, I didn't mean to scare you. I just need to talk to you."

"Whew! Your call nearly gave me a heart attack. Don't scare me like that. With your kind of job—"

"I'm sorry. When can I see you?"

"Where are you now?"

"I'm downtown," I responded.

"Wilmington?"

"Yeah."

"Wonderful! I'm at The Pilot House. Come on over." I snapped the phone shut, looking up the hill at the restaurant, only a couple of blocks away. I drove around the blocks and climbed the interior staircase as Pepper ran to meet me.

"I can't believe it! I didn't expect to see you today," she said glancing at my too-casual attire. "Come and meet Saul."

I stopped in my tracks. "Pepper, I have to talk to you. Now! You didn't say you'd brought him with you."

"What difference does that make? You need to meet him anyway."

She dragged me to where her fiancé sat, the table barely large enough to accommodate two people much less three.

"Saul, this is Logan Hunter, the friend I told you about. She's going to be my attendant." The man grinned. "It's a pleasure to meet you." He threw out his hand and I ignored it.

"I've seen you before. Here at the harbor." I wanted to put the screws to him, my tone unfriendly.

His face flushed. "Well, I suppose you could have. I do come down to The Riverwalk occasionally. I live on Third Street so it's convenient to walk down on lovely evenings."

He knew damn well I'd seen him. I wanted to interrogate him and spill my guts to Pepper about his boarding *Fearsome Ferry*, but not now. I needed to get Pepper away from him, but how?

Pepper grinned. "Let's move to a bigger table and Logan can join us, Saul."

"No, thanks. I'm not dressed for dinner. I'm working on a case. I have to go."

"Is this the same case you've been working on down here?"

"Uh, yeah, but I can't discuss it, Pepper, and you shouldn't either." Pepper gave me a strange look. "I have to go, but I seriously need to talk to you soon, in private."

I leaned toward Saul. "If anything happens to Pepper, I'll come looking for you. She doesn't deserve to be mistreated."

He pulled his shoulders back in shock.

Pepper, noticeably stunned by my outburst, snatched my arm. "Logan! What on earth is wrong with you?"

"I can't explain it right now, Pepper. Just be sure to call me later."

I hugged her and whispered for her to be careful. I bounded down the stairs and around the dark corner toward the Hummer, feeling this trip had been worthless.

Shit! Now Pepper would tell Turrentine I'm an SBI agent. If he were involved in the porn business beyond being a "guest," he would be on the alert from now on. I called in to headquarters to request cell phone records and signal-tower information for Saul Turrentine and Thomas Irving Trollinger. Those records would show where they were at the time of Maeve's death and how fast they were moving, walking, or driving. I just needed to call them "persons of interest" in the case.

I parked on Orange St. and eased down the dark brick street and around the corner toward the depot. The same woman stood guard. Unhappy to see me, she threatened, "I'm notifying the owner about you. You've already been told to go away."

"Sorry, ma'am, but I think my husband is cheating on me," I lied. "I want to confirm it so I can ruin his ass."

The woman's face softened a bit, but she didn't let me board. I kicked pebbles and headed up the street, stopping in front of the Suck, Bang, Blow store, the store whose name was written on a note stuck under my windshield wiper.

Wait a minute! Do I see costumes in there behind the paper products and balloons?

It wasn't even close to Halloween. On closer observation, it seemed to be a year-round store with not only paper party products but also the makings of interesting disguises. I had to wonder if some of the ferry crowd were regular customers. Hadn't one of the girls I questioned mentioned a videographer with bad hair or a possible wig?

I walked inside and studied the four walls, pulling together an outfit of my own: brunette shoulder-length wig, a maid's black-and-white mini-dress with a ruffle back panty, four-inch spectator stilettos—not official agency attire, but I intended to go under cover like McCracken. The way-too-short dress and dangerously high heels should throw off suspicion.

~~~~~

The heaviness of the air at Carolina Beach drew my eyes up. Ten o'clock in the morning but the sky darkened and thunder rumbled from a distance. Not good. At least two miles from my vehicle, no rain gear, no protection whatsoever.

Clap!

Lightning approached. I pulled the binoculars over my head and started jogging. The ocean slapped waves onto the shore relentlessly. The sea grass bowed all the way to the blowing sand. I picked up speed, pushing my legs into high gear as pea-sized hail pelted me. No houses or piers to duck under, just me against the storm. I ran at a fast clip, making out the silhouette of my Hummer still far away.

Clap!

"Ouch!" The hail, larger now, stung my head and skin as I stayed away from the one lone scrubby tree while the lightning closed in. The wet sand pulled on my feet, slowing my pace, but when the hail reached golf ball size, I flew to the rocking Hummer. The windshield cracked as I dove into the back and cowered to wait for Mother Nature to calm down.

Hail bruises—a new experience for me. I would mend, but the Hummer had to go in for a new windshield. Witnesses reported a large waterspout offshore and if it had come ashore, it would have been considered a small tornado. I didn't care. Nothing could ruin my mood. I was meeting Chase to catch him up on the investigation—and a few other things.

He ran to meet me as I stepped out, wringing wet.

"Logan, what on earth happened?"

I reached for him and wrapped my lips around his, trying to speak at the same time.

"Hail...water spout...Ow!"

Chase pulled away.

"Just a few bruises. The storm caught me out in the open too far from the Hummer." Chase glanced at the Hummer and back at me. "Let's get inside, dry you off, and doctor those bruises."

I hopped into the tiny shower in Chase's motel room where he would be practically camping out while he did surveillance on ICW activities and the mouth of the Cape Fear River below Fort Fisher. When I emerged, Chase kissed my bruises—every one of them—several times. During the hours we had off the clock, we stayed wrapped in each other's arms, rekindling the passion that had evaded us over the past few weeks. And with his mother's funeral and subsequent legal work behind him, we could now get back to work on the same investigation.

"God, I've missed you so much," Chase purred into my sore ear. "Let's make a pact to stick together like glue from now on."

"Nothing would suit me better. Now if we can convince Poletti that we're inseparable."

"Yeah. Fat chance of that, but he's not deliberately trying to keep us apart."

"I know. He's really been wonderful, coming to our wedding, and giving you so much time off even if he couldn't do the same for me."

Chase, always the realist, frowned. "Well, with the economy like it is, he's likely to pull one of us somewhere else."

"I don't want to talk about that, Chase. Get over here!"

He was on me like white on rice and I loved it, the bruises numbed by some fragrant ointment he'd rubbed all over me.

When Chase and I surfaced again, we were famished and headed to the Tuscan Grill where we promptly filled our empty hollows. We shared the best meal either of us had eaten in a long time. Once we satisfied our appetites, we discussed murder investigations.

Chase sank back into his chair. "I'm doing some surveillance of *Cat Eyes.*"

"What's that? It sounds like a song title."

"Actually it's a catamaran tour company. It takes folks down the waterway and into inlets and coastal towns to do some shopping. But here's the deal: apparently the high-speed catamarans also do a little sleazing on the side."

"Like what?"

"I popped into that bar beside the motel last night and overheard a conversation. Seems the drunk had just come off a catamaran that took him out to a ferry for 'the time of his life.'"

"*Fearsome Ferry?*"

"He didn't call it that, but I'm assuming so."

"That fits with what McCracken told me. He said he'd seen catamarans taking people from Bald Head to the ferry."

"I guess they have a solution for every problem. It's certainly frustrating as hell to law enforcement."

"Those sleaze bags have a sophisticated operation even if their clients aren't sophisticated at all."

"Yeah, since the ferry moves into the sound and away from prying eyes, it figures they've got some way to get the traffic out to them wherever they are."

"And it's a huge ferry, Chase. It looks like a renovated car ferry and you know how big those things are."

"You're exactly right about that, Logan. I asked the drunk about it and he spouted off plenty. He said it had once been a Great Lakes car ferry and somebody renovated it into a three-story porn palace."

"Well, it doesn't always stay away from prying eyes, because I've seen it pull right in to that depot downtown where *The Henrietta III* docks and board people."

"What's *The Henrietta III?*"

"A wonderful riverboat with a paddle wheel. I think it's the largest one in North Carolina. It takes people down the Cape Fear River for dinner and dancing, mostly on Friday and Saturday nights. When it's out, it's gone for about three hours. It's perfectly legit. My theory is that the depot lady has been paid off to take care of *Fearsome Ferry* when they brazenly come to The Riverwalk. They have it worked out so that the ferry comes in while the riverboat is out. I feel sure that *The Henrietta* owners wouldn't approve of this activity and wouldn't want to be associated in any way. I'm looking forward to taking Miss Depot down with the rest of the porn operation."

"I imagine the riverboat owners will be glad when that day comes."

"It can't be soon enough to suit me."

19

Dock Street seemed darker than usual and I felt very much alone, Chase following a catamaran miles away and McCracken who knew where. The other streets had old-fashioned streetlights that added to the ambience of the downtown waterfront, and they were here too, just not on. Even if shops were closed, people often strolled the attractive brick streets and occasionally a horse-drawn buggy would go by carrying a couple back to the Hilton after a dinner or a tour of historic homes.

I was disappointed Two Sisters Bookery had closed for the night. Not that I had time to read, but I liked having a few books around in case I found some time. I could hear music all the way to Fifth Street where I knew The Cape Fear Blues Jam was in full swing. Even with the music tonight, the street I'd parked on gave me an uncomfortable feeling. Incredibly dim. I looked behind me and vaguely made out a silhouette in the mist. Probably some other poor soul, wishing his vehicle was closer.

I stuck my hands in my pockets, but before I had my fingers around my gun, something bumped hard, and I hit the brick, barely getting one hand out to help break the fall. I scampered to my feet in time to see a big man in a long swinging coat running hard away from me. I ran after him, but by the time I got to the corner, he'd disappeared. I heard more footsteps behind me and turned, my gun visible and ready.

McCracken touched my arm and then my face. "You okay?"

"I'm fine." I wrenched away from him and refocused on the streets. There weren't many people milling about and only one shop remained open: Suck, Bang, Blow. The hulking man who hit me had to be inside. I thought McCracken would follow me in, but he disappeared as quickly as he'd materialized.

When I made my way to the back of the store, I looked under the dressing-room door where I'd tried on disguises. I saw nothing, so I moved on. The door behind me burst open and powerful arms grabbed me around the neck, a hand smothering my mouth. I'm tall but no match for this kind of brut force. He tossed me around, choking me, my legs swinging while I tried to figure a way to bring him down, the gun in my pocket out of reach, my arms flailing and beating the big bruiser.

Think. Think! Where the hell is McCracken?

The store clerk ran into the hallway, and the goon abruptly slammed me into the wall and bolted out the alley exit.

"What the hell? You're bleeding," the store clerk said, McCracken now peering over her shoulder. I looked down at my knees, both skinned and bleeding.

"What happened to you?"

"Get the hell out of my way, you two!" I pushed them both and darted out the door, catching only a glimpse of a large silhouette way down the street past The Reel Café.

McCracken ran up behind me, at least I hoped it was McCracken. I glanced around, relieved to see him. We rounded Orange Street and saw the large figure duck into The Cape Fear Serpentarium, an enclosed reptile park.

As we dashed in the front lobby, a wide-eyed man ran toward us. "We're getting ready to close." But he slammed on brakes when he saw our weapons.

"SBI. Did a big man just come in?"

"I didn't see anybody. Like I said, we're closing. We never let people in when we're feeding serpents."

"Lock up," I called out to him, "but we're searching this whole place if we have to."

He nodded and disappeared.

McCracken and I heard a commotion at the same time and picked up speed, passing display after display of slithering serpents—hungry and agitated slithering serpents—each in a Plexiglas case of natural habitat.

"Hey!" someone hollered.

I looked down the corridor as the big goon hit a man feeding a Komodo dragon. The lid slid open, and with surprising swiftness, the worlds' largest lizard made a break, heading straight for us. We were closed in to a narrow space on both sides, our guns drawn, looking at each other questioningly. Do we shoot the monitor? My clammy hand made my gun slippery, but I managed to hang on to it by wrapping my finger through the trigger space.

"Don't shoot it!" somebody yelled from our right. "He won't hurt you."

McCracken and I backed up as the giant monitor continued to *swish-swash* in our direction, flicking its reptilian tongue. We got to the end of the hallway and I veered off to the left as McCracken went right. I looked back at the wide-eyed man from the lobby, my attacker nowhere in sight.

"Agents," the manager called to us, "that guy's on the second level."

I ran to the stairwell and McCracken rode the elevator, hoping to end any plan the man had of escaping. McCracken stepped off the elevator and we nodded and circled the floor in opposite directions as the ceiling lights dimmed.

"Hey!" I heard McCracken call out, "turn the lights up, not down!"

Silence.

I eased along, waving my weapon into every path between serpent displays, hearing my own breath, feeling the *thump-thump* of an uneasy heart, sweat dripping from every pore on my body. I didn't like serpents, especially in near darkness.

That's when I heard the stair door slam many yards behind me.

"Shit! He slipped by us," I called to McCracken, who didn't respond.

"McCracken?"

"Hunter, freeze where you are."

"What? We have to get after him, damn it! What's—"

"Big guy left us a present," McCracken whispered. I could see sweat glistening on his face. I advanced another step. "Freeze, damn it!"

Then I saw movement on the floor—a deadly Bushmaster snake, at least twelve feet long. I froze, but I couldn't help jumping a few seconds later when a loud siren went off, further unraveling my nerves as the elevator door opened and three frantic men in brown uniforms rushed out.

"Don't kill it!"

McCracken and I retreated rapidly to the elevators and got the hell out of the building. Once back out on Orange Street, there was no sign of my attacker.

~~~~~

I drove home and doctored my knees, angry I hadn't caught up with the big thug. I didn't even get a good look at him except for his noticeably long hair swishing as he ran away from me. I wouldn't sleep much, wondering how close McCracken had been to me when I crashed into the sidewalk. Had he seen the assailant in time to stop the attack? Or had he been as surprised as I was?

As I put away the first-aid kit, my thoughts settled once more on my friend. I worried about Pepper. What had she gotten herself into with the Turrentine man?

~~~~~

Rain set in for the day. The morning streets were inactive, but more tourists and regulars came out in the afternoon to lunch along the river's edge. I'd chosen a bistro table on a street near Chandler's Wharf underneath a market umbrella, where I ordered a glass of lemonade and a half-sandwich.

Two girls who looked to be in their late teens giggled a few tables down, one of them getting wet since the canopy didn't extend as far as her chair. It didn't seem to bother her. I sipped my drink and let my eyes go from one end of the brick street to the other. Not a sign of anyone I recognized.

I turned my head as the girls splashed through puddles to catch a van that had pulled within a few yards of Ann Street. As the van sped away, I saw its side: The Flash Van painted in neon colors for all to see. How blatant can you get? But then, how many people really knew what went on inside this particular van? Most tourists and regulars saw a standard van, not the porn factory I knew was inside.

I had two choices: get to the Hummer several blocks away and try to catch up with it or stay put until it dropped the girls off later. I stayed put but moved inside Elijah's and found a window so I could see out and not be so easily seen.

An hour and twenty-two minutes later, I heard the girls talking loudly outside the building, the van nowhere in sight. I approached them. "Excuse me. Where's the van that's supposed to be here?"

They looked at each other, shrugged, and the blonde answered. "It dropped us off. Why?"

"Well, I hoped to get on it," I lied. "I've tried three damn times to catch it. I need the money bad."

"Really? Wow, I know the men will like those long legs of yours. You could wrap them around some of those little pricks twice. And you're so pretty, you know, for your age." Yikes! I suddenly felt ancient at thirty years old.

The other girl nudged her hard. "Come on. I gotta get this money in the bank today. My tuition's due."

"You go ahead. I'm hungry. I'll catch up later." The girl shrugged again and walked off.

I took the opportunity to ask the blonde to sit with me. She seemed willing to talk. "So you were on The Flash Van?"

"Uh, yeah." She glanced around her. "You're not a cop, are you?"

"Hell no," I said, hoping my lie wasn't transparent.

"I've been on it twice now. Easy money, only..."

"Only?"

"Well, don't get me wrong, I enjoy sex, but sometimes it's awful rough. These guys today wanted us to do stuff we've never done before. To each other. Too weird."

"And you did?"

"What's the big deal? It doesn't matter, does it? I need money. Tuition keeps going up. It's the fastest way I know to get a grand in the hand."

"Wow! What do I have to do to get on the damn thing?"

"They go around looking for girls. Sometimes married women get on. I guess they're bored or need the money. All you gotta do is hang out down here and those creeps will check you out. A thousand dollars comes in handy. You're pretty. They'll pick you up and drop you back off in a couple of hours."

"Is it always the same men?"

"How should I know? What difference does it make?"

"Do they wear condoms?"

She laughed loud. "No, they just *do* you, sometimes two at a time, like today."

"Don't you worry about where their dicks have been?"

"Like I said, what's the difference? And," she said, standing over me, "you ask too many damn questions. I'm outta here." She shoved her money in her pocket, and her dangerous stilettos clicked away from me down the sidewalk.

20

Finally on *Fearsome Ferry* with a bogus work pass and in my maid costume, I intended to have a look around. It was full of people, many young beautiful half-dressed girls and boys who didn't look much over eighteen, along with plenty of men and women my age or older. They doted on each other rather than paying any attention to me, my new mini-revolver, a .22 Mag Black Widow, loaded and barely hidden beneath my short wait-staff uniform. Fortunately the weapon only weighed nine ounces. I adjusted my wig and tottered along on high heels.

The ferry divided into levels, the first a bar and numbered private rooms. I picked up a tray with a pitcher of ice water and four glasses and went to the room farthest from me. I knocked and opened the door enough to slip in. Hot lights and cameras spotlighted young girls posing in various stages of undress and in various positions with their tiny boobs pointed as far out as possible and their bodies contorted to look as sexy as possible. Heavy makeup made them appear years older than they probably were. Most of them seemed apprehensive, but the cameraman, no doubt experienced at soothing and flattering, got the poses he wanted. He gestured toward me from behind the camera.

"Thanks for the water. Okay, ladies, take a break and wet those lips. Five minutes."

The videographer walked to the opposite corner while they grabbed glasses. I filled them and left the room with the empty tray, never getting a good look at him.

Several rooms appeared to be studios like the one I'd just left. I moved past them to a door ajar, where I could see a naked man on a bed with a nearly nude girl. She whimpered while he tried to coax her into having sex, maybe for the first time. She told him 'no', and I was relieved when he backed off and didn't force her. I pushed the door and a weird-looking cameraman appeared.

"Do you need some water?"

"Water? Hell no! Get the hell away from here!" He slammed the door in my face.

I needed to get off this level before I aroused too much suspicion, but I really wanted to help that poor girl without blowing my cover. Hopefully the men would leave her alone. I got nauseated anyway, from the room reeking of incompatible odors fighting each other: lavender, rose, cinnamon, vanilla, and recent sex. I gagged, opened the only window in the walkway, and took my heels and skirt to another level of wickedness.

Guests on the second level—one huge room— apparently didn't feel they needed privacy. Smells of sweaty sex hit my nostrils hard. The sight, a smorgasbord of sex— any kind, any one—no holds barred. Messy beds everywhere, some with gays pounding each other, some with lesbians and dildos. I took a step back. No, not a dildo—a large green zucchini! A huge round bed took center stage under a mirror ball with a twisting orgy in full throttle. Of course, strategically positioned cameras filmed the acts from every angle. I gulped, feeling uncomfortable and wanting to leave before someone tried to drag me into the reckless decadence.

I took a short spiral staircase to the top level of the ferry. All doors were closed, but I could hear cracks of whips and cries of pain—or did they call it ecstasy? A woman appeared down the corridor in a black leather bikini bottom, her breasts wrapped with leather strips threaded through metal bars in each nipple. She had jet-black hair, heavy black eye makeup, and blood red lips. I supposed it showed up well on camera. Much to my relief, she went into a room and closed the door behind her.

The remaining remnants of my comfort level disintegrated. Sex on this level had to be hard-core: S and M, bondage, and no telling what else. I took a deep breath and turned the knob on a door, vowing to get off *Fearsome Ferry*. What I saw shocked me. A woman about my age writhed on the bed with a man's arm up to his elbow inside her. I'd heard of fisting, but the sight? Unbelievable. A videographer perched almost on top of them. I pulled the door closed and tried to catch my breath as a deranged man ran by me with an IV line dangling from one of his red bulbous testicles.

All restraint, all boundaries, all limitations had been checked at the boarding ramp. Rampant perversion. Nearly every sin listed in The Ten Commandments played out on this sleaze ship. I, only an observer, felt filthy. I headed down the stairs with nausea hitting me in waves. When I reached the first level, a large black plastic bag appeared in my face.

"Here, get this garbage to the Dumpster. And hurry back. People are thirsty."

I nodded, took the bag, pitching it into the Dumpster as I realized the ferry was nowhere close to any land. I couldn't get off! I puked over the metal rail, watching the stream of spew hit the water below. I eased around the deck, trying to stay under the second-floor deck until I spotted an inflatable lifeboat tied to the side. I crouched to untie it so I could get away. I'd had enough, and it was dark as four feet up an alligator, so maybe I could sneak away without notice.

I worked quietly to get the boat in the water without noise and had eased myself into it when I heard feet running down the deck. Some dude came straight at me, and hurtled himself into the rubber boat with enough force to make it shoot into the air and nearly catapult me into the river. The little boat belched as soon as he landed on my four-inch heel.

"What the hell?" I cowered, taking in a nasty-looking pirate on steroids who invited himself into my getaway boat.

"Shhhh!"

I could hear more running as the pirate and I both grabbed oars and paddled into the river's darkness.

When I felt comfortable that we were out of earshot, I began my rant.

"How dare you shush me! Who do you think you are?"

His head, wrapped in a purple East Carolina do rag, covered most of his hair. He held a tiny penlight to his face.

"Hunter? Your hair..."

"McCracken, what are you doing here?" I didn't know whether to be relieved or alarmed.

"I came to help you, gift-wrapped," he grinned, pulling off the headgear.

"Some gift." I didn't mean to say that out loud, but there it was.

"No appreciation. None at all. However, I see you're gift-wrapped too. I likey." He crammed the rag in his pocket along with his demeanor. "You were about to get yourself in big trouble. And, by the way, I thought we were going to work together on this case."

"You obviously haven't been working with me." He stayed quiet. I sighed. "Okay, I suppose neither of us is cooperating with the other."

"You think?" He looked around and pulled out the penlight again. "Not much, but it beats total darkness."

"My feet are wet!"

He shone the light into the boat, now filling with water.

"Shit!" we said simultaneously.

"Hope you can swim, Hunter." I could, but the thought of alligators made me cringe.

We were both in the drink soon enough, McCracken trying to shine his pitiful excuse for a light around, hoping to find a land mass big enough for the two of us.

"There! Swim for those trees."

The trees seemed miles away, but what choice did we have? If we tired, the river current could sweep us into the Atlantic Ocean not much farther downstream.

Breathless, we pulled ourselves out of the river, through mud, and up beside a couple of scraggily trees to lean on. We sat there for a while as our breathing leveled off, McCracken shining the penlight around to get his bearings.

I shivered.

"You all right?"

"Yeah."

More silence.

"Your teeth are chattering. Let me warm you up," he said, sliding his arm around my back.

"I'm fine!" I slipped out of his grasp.

"All right!" he yelled back. "Just don't get far away. I'd hate to see a gator take off one of those long legs of yours."

I slid back over. "Do you really think they're some here?"

"Hunter, please. Alligator Creek flows into the Cape Fear. Do you really think gators just stay in the creek? They'll go wherever there's food."

I didn't want to be food.

"There's really nothing we can do until it gets light and we can figure out where we are. Not big enough to be Eagle Island. Could be Keg Island. Don't suppose you have a phone or radio on you?"

"No." But I did have a small gun attached to my ruffle-back panty. I reached under my skirt and touched an empty holster. "Shit!"

"That seems to be your favorite word."

"Well, that's what we're mired in, and it's deep. And besides, that gun was brand new!"

"Could be worse."

"How?"

"Well," he squirmed around toward me, "we could have been shot, or drowned, or eaten by—"

"Okay! Your point is well-taken."

"Don't ever let your guard down. That's when you get hurt."

"Ah, SBI manual, page seven."

"I'm serious. You let your guard down, Hunter."

Maybe I had. I got caught up in all the filthy activities around me on the ferry, but I wasn't about to admit that to Mr. Know-it-all.

"Are you speaking from experience? You know, about letting your guard down?"

"Damn right."

Silence set in again. Stars pricked the sky, and I calmed myself by taking in the distant lighted church steeples of downtown Wilmington, trying to forget about the mess we were in—until I heard McCracken snoring. How could he sleep out here, not knowing what lurked behind trees or at the edge of the Cape Fear River? I sat motionless.

At least one of us will get some rest.

~~~~~

I welcomed the first hint of sunrise, watching as it spread across water and lit the day. I bent my knees and pulled them up to my chest to stretch before I stood. McCracken rustled beside me, his face near mine when one of his eyes popped open.

"Ahhh! Don't scare me like that so early in the morning!"

"Cute," I glowered at him. "You don't look so good yourself." I stirred. "I've got to move around."

"Me too."

We both stood and maneuvered around some trees, finding a clearing that had signs of partying: empty beer cans, several old campfire spots, and a few pieces of trash.

"Well, somebody knows where this place is."

"Keg Island. Not big enough to be Eagle."

I agreed, having previously studied a map of the Cape Fear River and learning there were a couple of islands in the middle of it. I checked sand for signs of alligators as McCracken pilfered around in some brush and came back with a partial bag of corn chips with ants. We flicked them off and shared the chips, our only nourishment, with nothing to wash them down.

As McCracken stood in front of me, I had to snicker at his open fly.

"The goat is leaving the pasture again," I smirked at him. "Can't you contain it?"

He glanced down, grabbed his zipper, and yanked it up.

"Hard to contain this rascal as large as it is."

"Ha! You're delusional! And I think you leave yourself unzipped on purpose."

"No, damn it, it's these cheap undercover clothes. Not the best coverage for ole Billy here," he grinned with more than a degree of pride. I wanted to make a few more comments about investing in Fruit of the Looms but zipped my lips instead.

We could see banks of the river on both sides, but neither of us suggested another swim. Hours passed as I spotted several nests of ibis along the banks, and the sun baked my skin crispy before a Cessna flew over. We hid at first, then realized it might be a Coast Guard search plane and waved and hollered until it disappeared, not sure if the pilot ever saw us. I didn't want to spend another night out here feeling as nervous as a bloodworm on a fishhook. I didn't want to go back in the water and I didn't want to be gator lunch. Another night was out of the question, so we made a plan.

McCracken went in one direction and I in another, hoping we could find a water-worthy vessel somewhere around Keg Island. Large raindrops suddenly came from straight over me and soaked my skimpy outfit, irritating me further. When we met later, neither of us had found anything, except McCracken who had a large tree limb.

"What are you planning to do with that thing?"

I heard a loud hiss behind me and turned to take in a monstrous reptile.

"Clobber that gator before he has a sexy maid for an afternoon snack. Big fellow too." McCracken pounded the alligator on the head until it gave up and slunk back into the water. I gulped. Had I stained my ruffle back panty? Amazingly I had not.

Silence returned for a while as we rested on hot sand, having no choice but to let relentless sun scorch us as we kept gators at bay. I pulled at the tiny skirt and wide low neckline to no avail. Since I was stuck on this island with a man I hardly knew, I interrogated him, as much for entertainment as anything else.

"How long you been in the field, McCracken?"

"With the bureau over fifteen years. In the field at first, then pushing a pencil for a while," he answered. I had noticed little threads of silver around his ears.

"Late bloomer, are you?"

"Not that it's any of your business, but they called it 'residual emotion.' I left the field after my wife died." His jaw quivered. "Just couldn't handle it."

"I'm sorry. I didn't know." If my skin hadn't already started to burn, my face would have turned red from awkwardness.

"Angie and I were both agents, working together on a case in Raleigh. We were hot on the trail. Then Angie's mother died suddenly and we headed to West Virginia with a few days off. A day after the funeral, we took a drive through the mountains with a picnic basket and some wine. Out of the blue, a truck rammed us hard from behind and sent us over an embankment. I walked away. She didn't. Killed on impact. When they closed the Raleigh case, turned out he bragged about following us up there and biding his time until we got into a remote area. Meant to get me too, of course, but instead he permanently wounded me. I've had to live with it."

"It's not your fault."

"How would you know?" he bellowed. "I should have realized an agent's never off-duty. I should have been able to keep the car from going over the mountain. I should have made her buckle up. I—" He shook his beet red face, got up, and stumbled off while I sat, speechless.

I checked the narrow island as the sun continued to bake my skin. I had no protection from it or from the enormous insects that swarmed down to attack every bare inch. I attempted to fend them off with my cheap wig.

When he returned a while later, McCracken seemed to be fine.

"I hope that pilot saw us," he said, breaking the awkwardness.

"Yeah, me too. Chase'll figure out I'm missing, but he doesn't know where to look."

"Isn't he over at Carolina Beach?"

"Only a few miles from us, but—"

We saw a speck of something in the water, heading in our direction.

"Somebody's coming! Maybe the pilot did see us after all."

"We'd better hope it's one of our guys," McCracken said.

We both locked our eyes on the water and watched the speedboat approach, the best-looking blonde I'd ever met waving as I waved back.

"Chase?"

"Chase," I answered, "my hero."

"You owe him a blow job."

I glared at the prick unable to come up with a snappy reply, glad Chase hadn't heard the comment. Otherwise McCracken might become McCrackedteeth.

The pilot *had* seen us, and Chase volunteered to pick us up so our identities would stay intact. I'm sure McCracken and I both smelled like scorched fish left in the sun too long. The afternoon was so humid I swear I could see moisture suspended in the air, but I didn't give a squirting shit. I limped to the boat, pissed, sore, and smelly but relieved to see Chase and get off the fricking island. Chase glared at me and gave my tiny outfit the once over without speaking. He never spoke about us being on the ferry and the island alone all night, one a pirate, and one a skimpily-clad barmaid.

~~~~~

Back at our condo I dabbed cream all over my sunburned face, arms, and legs, and broached the subject.

"I know you're upset with me."

"Logan, what were you thinking? First of all, you don't go into the enemy camp without backup, without reporting in, without... Are you listening to me?"

"Not if you're going to scold me." I walked into our kitchen, feeling his eyes boring holes in my back.

"Did it ever occur to you the danger you put yourself in? And Dick-for-brains didn't—"

"Chase, I'm fine. And I did have backup—sort of." I failed to mention that Dick, uh, McCracken and I didn't plan our encounter on the ferry or on the island.

Chase said a few choice words and went out on the condo's deck, slamming the door behind him. I poured two glasses of sweet iced tea and pushed the door open, handing him a glass as we stood at the railing that overlooked the sound. We sipped in silence before I slid over close enough to have our arms touch. He threw his arm around me and I looked up into those tanzanite eyes and melted into a puddle.

"Chase, I'm sorry I worried you."

"It's just that I love you so much, Logan. I couldn't deal with anything happening to you. I want to protect you, and well, damn it, I seldom see you. It seems that even when we're on the same case, we're not working together."

"As much as I adore the idea of your protecting me, I can take care of myself." He kissed my nose without disagreeing. "You're right. I do wish we could work closer together. Maybe when the recession is over." We kept having the same feeble conversation. "Anyway, we can get this case finished faster by splitting up, don't you think?"

"All I know is from now on I expect my tea served in the maid outfit."

Making up was beyond belief. Wonderful. Fulfilling. Passionate. Once Chase headed to the shower, I lay there, thinking about how lucky we were to have each other and to work together as much as we did. I got to experience making love—its physical give and take—with someone I truly loved, and hadn't been subjected to the kind of exercise in salaciousness I dealt with daily in this investigation.

I also thought about McCracken losing his wife. How awful his pain and guilt had to be. I seriously needed to be nicer to him and thank God every waking moment that Chase and I had each other to hold on to even if our assignments separated us.

21

I read the license plate on the cherry red Porsche Boxster in front of me: T I T 44DD. It had to be Trollinger's. I stayed parked since the street didn't have enough light to illuminate me at two o'clock in the morning. I soon heard voices and ducked as two figures strolled to the convertible, which started remotely, I supposed for fast getaways.

Once the car turned the corner, I eased out and followed. Tit drove and the woman pulled a scarf closer to keep it from blowing away. I followed the couple through the streets of Wilmington and into a familiar neighborhood.

The convertible pulled into the Beaujue-Dufour driveway and the woman leaned over and kissed Tit passionately, got out, and went inside. He backed out and sped down the road, apparently not noticing me at the opposite curb. I followed the car back to a riverfront condominium.

Tit and Antonella were closer than I'd been led to believe. Business partners? Lovers? I had more questions for Antonella, and it pissed me off to work so hard for so little information. I wanted to interrogate Trollinger and Roache.

I had plenty of evidence to tie them to pornography, but I really had nothing to connect them to Maeve's death. I would have to be patient. I needed more specific information before I confronted them.

22

Research turned up no live births for Celyn Manley who had never married, but adopted Bailey. She had lied about all of it, and because that lie might somehow have relevance to the case, it was time to engage in a meaningful conversation with her. I found her in the backyard. She had climbed a ladder with a drill in one hand and a metal sculpture in the other, trying to secure it to the exterior of the house. Her long flowing skirt seemed out of place for this project.

"Need some help?" I called out as I rounded the corner.

Ms. Manley glanced back. "Oh…yeah, thanks. I just bought this wonderful piece and thought I'd hang it before I change clothes." I held the ladder steady while she drilled the piece of sculpture into the mortar between two bricks. A gust of wind whipped her skirt up past my eye level. She had no free hand to pull it down. I stared as the skirt floated back down, revealing her alarmed face.

She descended, never once glancing in my direction. "I can't do this!"

"Uh…"

"I can't talk to you right now. Please go away!" She ran for the house as I stood still, not knowing what to say, but knowing what I saw.

~~~~~

I waited three days before approaching Celyn Manley again. I hadn't talked with Bailey and didn't intend to wait any longer, regardless of the obstacle. Apparently Celyn read the determination on my face. She pulled the door open and waved me in without a word.

When we reached the kitchen, she poured us both freshly brewed green tea, and we sat on the blue bar stools. She blushed. I needed to put her at ease, but the right words didn't come.

"Ms. Manley, I—"

"Agent Hunter, you know my secret. We need to talk about that. I know you're here to question Bailey, but, please... I need to explain some things. Will you let me send Bailey on an errand? Then I'll leave the two of you alone once she gets back."

"That's fine."

She called out to Bailey to go to the grocery store with a list, and told her she'd find the checkbook in the car. When Ms. Manley came back to me, I stayed at the kitchen window watching the purple Prius convertible roar away before she began her story.

"It's not that I'm a freak. I have Swyers syndrome. I'm called a male pseudohermaphrodite. If I were to totally undress, you'd see perky breasts and all the female genitalia."

"Ms. Manley, you don't have to—"

"Agent Hunter, let me finish this. Please. This is difficult enough without your constant interruptions." She cleared her throat. "I also have a penis. The medical community uses the term intersex. In most cases, the penis never descends. It stays inside, but the female doesn't have menstrual periods, so she can't bear children. Unfortunately, my penis descended enough that it's quite noticeable unless I'm careful how I dress. You found out when the wind blew my skirt the other day."

I nodded because my tongue stuck to the bottom of my mouth.

"I deal with it. My parents refused to make a decision at my birth, so I'm a female with extra equipment. I've never forgiven them. They should have let the doctors do something then. I don't date. I haven't been married, like I told you." She folded her hands in her lap and looked down.

"Ms. Manley, I'm not here to judge or ridicule. I don't intend to speak a word of this to anyone. It has nothing to do with my case. I certainly won't tell Bailey she's adopted."

Her head shot up. "Yes, my biggest fear is that Bailey will find out and never forgive me for all the lies I've made up over the years. But I've been a good mother, Agent Hunter. Except, well, hell, when she was a child, I wouldn't let her sit in my lap. I always made excuses. Can you imagine not holding your baby in your lap? I've never let her see me undressed. I always feign extreme modesty and that I want her to be modest as well. I'm sure she thinks I'm very cold." She shifted her body. "In any case, I'm worried about her."

"First of all, I think you should be honest with Bailey. She's grown now and can probably handle it. After all, it's not your fault."

"Please don't get involved in that, Agent Hunter. Yes, I know I'll have to tell her at some point, but not right now. Please tell me why you're here."

"Bailey is on the list with many other girls who knew Maeve Smoltz. Some of them have been involved in Internet porn."

"Oh, my God, no! I knew Antonella was bad news."

"Antonella?"

"I think she's talked Bailey into doing something she shouldn't. Is that right?"

"I'm not sure how Antonella and Bailey are involved, and I'm not saying Bailey participated in pornography, Ms. Manley. In fact, I've been told she didn't, but she knows many people in the business. I've seen her with Tit. His real name is Tommy Trollinger."

"Yes, I've heard of Tommy. In fact, he picked her up in his black Jaguar for the funeral. I didn't understand why she wanted to go. She barely knew the girl. Or, at least, that's what she told me."

"I thought Trollinger drove a red car."

"He must have more than one, Agent Hunter. Bailey did tell me that he's filthy rich."

"That may be the case."

Definitely filthy.

Bailey Manley returned and her mother offered us more sweet tea behind the house where lush shrubs and colorful bushes framed two purple Adirondack chairs. Bailey's hair was as wiry and wild as the first time I'd seen her at Maeve's funeral—a pretty girl with a pleasant demeanor but no smile.

"Bailey, I understand you knew Maeve Smoltz."

"Uh huh."

"I need to know how well."

"We both went to New Hanover High School and then to UNCW. We weren't friends, but we had classes together. She was quiet and shy in high school. Me too. I still am."

"But she changed?"

"Yes, ma'am," she said before gulping some tea. "I don't know what happened to her, but she got wild the first semester. She hung all over boys. I heard she propositioned a professor and he reported it, but I don't know if that's true."

"Did you socialize with her?"

"No."

"Then why is your name and number in her cell phone journal?"

"What? Why would she do that?"

"I'm asking you. You must have socialized with her at least a little."

Bailey squirmed and tried to suck the bottom out of her glass.

"I can take you downtown for questioning if you don't feel comfortable talking here."

"No, please!" She stood and paced inside the shrub bed area for a few minutes.

"Did you ever go on *Fearsome Ferry*?"

"No."

"But you know what it is."

"Yes."

"Did you ever go on The Flash Van?"

"No!"

"Why not?"

"Why not? Because I'm not like that. I don't do stuff like that, Agent Hunter."

"Talk to me, Bailey. Stop making this so difficult. I'm tired of the games. I'm not leaving until I'm satisfied with your story."

Several sighs later, Bailey sat down.

"I've never been on the ferry or the van. I'd heard too much about them. I didn't want any part of it. But I went to one of the bathrooms on campus one afternoon and Maeve came out of a stall, all disheveled and grinning. I asked her what was going on since she looked kinda weird."

"What do you mean?"

"Her blouse was half-buttoned. I looked around to see if she'd been in the stall with somebody else, but nobody followed her out. She closed her phone and said 'phone sex is so rewarding.'"

"So she introduced you to phone sex."

"Yeah. I knew better, Agent Hunter, but she said it was fun, easy money, and no one could get hurt. She showed me how to get started. I got a 900 number and a camera phone and it was a piece of cake. I did it late at night so my mother wouldn't get wise."

"Texting?"

"Sometimes, but more often they wanted to hear me talking and breathing. It was hotter for both of us, you know?"

I didn't. "Are you still doing it?"

"No, I swear to you I'm not. I threw my phone in the Cape Fear River after Maeve died and cancelled that account. I don't ever intend to get involved with something like that again."

I stood. "I guess that's all I need for now. I may have more questions as the investigation progresses."

"Are you going to tell my mother?"

"I'll leave that unpleasant chore to you."

23

While *Fearsome Ferry* docked at a private pier in the marsh near The Cape Golf and Racquet Club, Chase and I, dressed in wait-staff attire—mine accessorized with yet another mini-revolver—managed to get on board, he heading in one direction and I in another. I walked toward a corridor, smugly thinking how easy that had been—until a man bumped me hard. *Not that again.* I looked up into the face of Pepper's fiancé, Saul Turrentine. *Oops!*

He took a step back and I tried to go around him. He caught my arm.

"Well, well. Agent Hunter. I suppose you and I need to talk, don't we?" He pushed me back toward the entrance. "It's not what you think."

Right. I nodded, without giving Chase away.

"We need to talk, but not here. You could be in danger. I heard them talking about the law being after them. We're getting off," Turrentine said.

"No. We, ah, I can't. I have to stay—"

He started to push me again, and I reached for my revolver.

"Hey! What's going on down there?" I saw Trollinger at the other end of the ferry and ducked my head behind Turrentine.

"I said 'what's going on down there?'" I could hear Trollinger walking toward us.

"Oh, this waitress is puking her guts out. I'm taking her off. Somebody'll have to double up tonight, I suppose."

"Damn!" The voice turned as he went in the opposite direction. "I'll take care of it."

"I just saved you," Turrentine whispered in my ear. I had thoughts of cinder block sandals weighting me to the bottom of the Cape Fear River. Where had Chase gone? I needed to at least signal him, but he was nowhere in sight.

Turrentine and I jumped off the ramp as it started to move into the ferry's bowels. Engines pulled the three-story vessel away from the pier as I stood there, aware Chase remained on it without me.

"How about a drink?"

"How can you be so cool with all you're involved in?"

"You don't know what's going on."

"I know plenty, Mr. Turrentine."

He sighed, and started to walk away.

"Wait a damn minute! You forced me off the ferry and now you're walking away?" I snatched up my gun. "You obviously don't know me very well."

He turned and stared at my drawn weapon, his mouth unhinging.

"Hold on now." He put his hands in the air. "I'm not a criminal. I just wanted to fill you in on a few things you don't understand."

"I understand plenty, mister."

"I somehow doubt that, Agent Hunter. No offense intended. Really. Look, follow me. Let's go somewhere you'll feel more comfortable."

Since I needed to contact Chase without this man's knowledge, I agreed. As I drove, I texted Chase to let him know I had been removed from the ferry and he was on his own. I'd drive back to wait for him once I talked to Turrentine. I got no text in return. Maybe good, maybe not.

Turrentine and I found a booth in a dark corner of the only dive within miles.

"You're an investor in *Fearsome Ferry*."

"No."

"You're a participant in porn."

"Well…"

"It's either yes or no. No 'wells' here," I said with a cold tone.

"I'd like to tell you why I'm involved."

"Oh, I can figure that out." I said, pulling at my short skirt.

"You're smart, Agent Hunter, but you don't understand."

"I can't wait to hear how you justify all this."

"My justification is my daughter." He ran his fingers through his thinning hair. "She's been missing for three months."

"You have a daughter?"

He nodded and pulled out a pack of cigarettes, offering me one.

"No, thanks, and I wish you wouldn't smoke in front of me."

"You're a bitch, you know that?" He stuck the smoke back in the pack and returned it to his pocket with a smirk.

"Thanks for the compliment. Now, what about your daughter, if you really have one?"

He pulled out his wallet to show me a picture of a woman with jet-black hair and garden green eyes.

"Laila, youngest of two children. I also have a son."

"So you have a daughter named Laila Turrentine."

"No, Laila Makatura. She married this Oriental guy she met at UNCW. Head over heels for him. I liked him okay. I mean, he was nice-looking, neat, planning to become an engineer once he completed the program at State."

"So she's married."

"Her husband was called home because of ailing parents, both terminal, I believe. She never heard from him again. She was frantic. I hired a private detective to find his sorry ass. He did. The guy went home and died. Massive heart attack at age of twenty-nine. I saw a copy of the death certificate, so it's legit."

He turned and motioned for a waiter. "I gotta have something strong. You want something? This story will take a while." He managed a sad smile and ordered whiskey and potato skins for both of us. I wondered how Chase was fairing on *S.S. Wicked*.

"Mr. Turrentine, I don't have time for this! I'm in the middle of an investigation you're screwing up."

"This story may help your investigation, Agent Hunter. Please hear me out." He shifted in his seat. "Laila went to pieces. I think she had a nervous breakdown, but doctors never called it that. They filled her with anti-depressants and told her to get on with her life. She moped around, couldn't work, couldn't eat or sleep, and then, all of a sudden she seemed happier. She said she'd taken back her maiden name. I thought she'd met someone nice, and everything would be fine."

"Mr. Turrentine—"

"Listen to me, Agent Hunter. She spent more time with Tobias—Toby—my son who's... well, he's retarded. He lives in a group home at the end of Castle Street, near the bridge. My brother, Paul, manages the home. I'd go visit him often, or call Paul to get a progress report on him. As long as Toby takes his meds, he's fine, but he's always been headstrong, and sometimes he refuses to cooperate. Toby's a big fella. My brother is no match for him physically, so he has to outsmart him. Someone at the group home—a nurse, I think—monitors the meds.

"Anyway, Toby got so complacent and depressed last year that I begged one of the town council members to give him a carriage tour job. The other two men are much more experienced and taught Toby how to take care of his horse and the tourists."

I glanced at my watch, needing to get back to Chase on the ferry. "Look, Mr. Turrentine, what has all this got to do with—"

"It's complicated. Paul called me one day and said Toby's testosterone was raging and he'd started touching women inappropriately on the carriage rides and might be fired. Paul and I sat down with Toby and told him he'd lose his job if he kept on. Toby said he understood, but a few days ago Paul told me he thinks Toby sees a lot downtown and knows sex goes on in the van, and he's probably heard some passengers talk about the ferry as well. Paul thinks Toby's been on the ferry." He shook his head. "How a big lug like him got on without being noticed beats the hell out of me."

I took my hand off the revolver I handled under the table. "A big lug?"

"Oh, I don't mean to put him down. He's just a huge man."

For the first time, Mr. Turrentine had my full attention. "Maybe somebody invited him as a joke. Or they wanted to see him in action. I don't know."

I thought about the rape video I'd seen, still unaware of where it had been filmed. The rapist's face had never been shown, but he was a huge, violent man. Could this have been Toby?

"I don't know about any of that, but I seem to have two children involved with that damn ferry." He guzzled his whiskey. "Anyway, I didn't mean to get off Laila. I was glad she spent some time with Toby, and maybe that satisfied her, you know, to pay some attention to him. He is manic-depressive, and only seems to be subdued when he's maneuvering tourists around in one of those carriages. That's the only thing he looks forward to. He gets to wear a top hat and cloak."

"A cloak?"

"Yes, all the drivers wear them."

"Does your son have long hair?"

"Well, it's longer than most, I suppose. Why?"

"Just curious. A large man in a cloak knocked me down a few nights ago."

"I hope it wasn't Toby. He is a big klutz, though."

"This was deliberate, believe me."

"Then I wouldn't suspect Toby." Turrentine leaned toward me. "Anyway, I was wrong about Laila. She'd been sitting down at the harbor, you know, just sitting there, staring off into space. Not doing anything wrong. But the owner of another restaurant told me after she disappeared that sometimes men would stop and chat, buy her a drink or something. Nothing wrong with that, I don't suppose. But one day he saw two men in a van approach her. That hippie van that's around all the time."

"The Flash Van?"

"You've done your homework. Anyway, she got on the van. I asked the owner if they dragged her or drugged her beforehand. He said she got up and willingly walked away with them."

"And you haven't seen her since?"

"Oh yeah. I told you this is a long story." He touched my arm and then drew it back. "It turns out she went on that damn van and did some pretty disgusting things, I'd imagine. I've done my homework too. They paid her and dropped her off. The restaurant owner said she kept coming back, waiting for them to pick her up again. And he said her skirts were shorter and her tops tighter with lots of cleavage. She's well-endowed, like her mother, rest her soul."

"Did they pick her up again?"

"Yeah, many times over a couple of months. Then someone got her on *Fearsome Ferry* and up to the third floor. Do you know what's on the third floor, Agent Hunter?"

"Hard core."

He choked back the pain. "My little girl doing God knows what, any time, anywhere. When I first got wind of it, I threatened to disown her if she ever got on the van or the ferry again. She left in a huff, slamming the door almost off its hinges. She said she had plenty of money for her own place and she was an adult. The whole drill. I haven't seen her since. Do you have any idea how that makes me feel? I may have made matters worse." His eyes filled with tears.

"I found out this guy named Tit is the main guy. At least, the most visible. He thinks he's immortal and all that, the arrogant son of a bitch."

"So, you're telling me you're here to find out what happened to your daughter, and you're not involved in the porn?"

He hung his head. "I can't say that exactly. Listen, I know this'll be hard to swallow, but hear me out. I'm afraid I *am* involved, in a way."

"I'm confused." We got another beverage and walked outside to a bistro table where I tried to text Chase again. Still no reply.

Damn!

"I got on the ferry with a work pass, like you. I hadn't planned to do anything, or anyone, just look around, try to find out if Laila—or Toby—were on there. I peeked in a door on the first floor where people posed for somewhat innocent-looking pictures in various stages of undress. Then I sat and talked to a pretty young thing in a private room for a while, just planning to find out if she knew Laila. I had a drink. One stinking drink! I'm a little emotional so I started crying and told her about Laila. She consoled me. Somehow I lost control. I'm not proud of it, Agent Hunter, but I found myself aroused. I had sex with that young girl. Younger than Laila, for Christ's sake. I went home feeling lower than an earth worm in shit." He shook his head.

"They probably slipped you some GHB. That seems to be how they overpower most unsuspecting people. Listen, I have to get back to…surveillance."

He paid no attention. "I went back again, fortifying myself that I wouldn't drink and I wouldn't have sex. I did fine until a woman came up to me and said 'Oh, you're the guy on the web site. Nice ass for your age.' I asked what she was talking about and she laughed and said to go to *Fearsome Ferry* web site and look. She couldn't believe I didn't know they filmed me having sex. I swear to you, Agent Hunter, I do have some self-respect and at least a little self control."

"So, are you on a porn site?"

"Hell yeah. Having sex. I had to be out of it. I vomited my guts out after I saw it. Then a waitress came with a tray of drinks. She asked if I needed Pepsi. I took one. I swear, I thought it was straight Pepsi this time."

"They tricked you a second time?"

He nodded. "Obviously I'm a very stupid man. Naïve, anyway. This time I was in an orgy on the second deck. Men! I'd never have sex with a man. I still puke over that." His voice filled with anger. "Do you believe any of this, Agent Hunter?"

"If you made this all up, you ought to be a writer."

"Tit knows me now. I've been on the ferry enough, involved in sex, and on the site. Hell, he thinks I love it. I've stopped drinking or eating anything, including water, but I have the advantage right now. I want to find out what happened to Laila. Now that other guy, Rude? He's mean. I hear he thinks he has a license to rape. He's the technician or whatever it's called."

"The webmaster?"

"Yeah. Rude designs and operates all of their Internet sites, but he has to answer to Tit. That much I'm sure of, even though Tit has trouble controlling that hothead."

"I know who you're talking about. Rude gives me the creeps too. Tit does seem to have some sense of decorum, at least."

"Yeah, but it's limited." He stopped and looked at me seriously. "I want to find my daughter." He leaned toward me.

"Look, I'll break it off with Pepper. She deserves better than me. I know that. She's a sweet lady. I might be infected, who knows? I need to come clean with her." His head hung. I remained silent. "She thinks you hang the moon, Agent Hunter."

"While we're being honest, do you love her?"

"Not really. We're both lonely. She's interesting, but I'm not sure I'd have made it to the altar, to be honest."

"Being lonely is no reason to sweep Pepper off her feet."

"You're right. I'll try to find the right words. I don't want to hurt her." He looked me dead in the eyes. "Agent Hunter, before you go, will you help me find Laila and find out if Toby is involved in this mess?"

"If you promise to stay out of the way. Don't come here anymore. Don't talk to Tit or Rude. Let us corral them and spring our trap."

"I'll try to stay out of your way."

"Let me make this a little clearer." I leaned in with a mean look. "Leave this to us, Mr. Turrentine."

"Please, after that lengthy story, call me Saul. And you might be able to find out some more about Tit by talking to Ms. Beaujue-Dufour."

"I've already talked to Antonella several times. She's not helpful."

"You misunderstand. I'm talking about Blaise Beajue-Dufour."

"You think she knows more than she's telling about the porn business?"

"Blaise and Tit are business partners and lovers. She supplied the money to move the operation from some dropout's van to the Internet. She's in it up to her deep throat."

I winced. So, that hadn't been Antonella all over Tit but her gorgeous mother instead. How had I missed all the signs?

~~~~~

I'd managed to plant a high-tech tracking device on the ferry before Saul grabbed me and escorted me off. The ferry, long gone by the time I left Saul, could still be tracked from the Hummer, but I had to find it and stay within range to follow it—no easy task. I stayed on roads as close to the river as possible, running into more than one dead end and then scrambling to pick up the *dot-beep* again. The ferry moved down the Cape Fear River and out into Masonboro Inlet.

When I finally collected Chase near daybreak, he was pissed because he'd ducked into a closet on the ferry and got locked in. He had learned absolutely nothing.

24

I followed Blaise Beaujue-Dufour, staying far enough behind not to be noticed in the shit wagon I'd borrowed from Crack, who was more than happy to drive the Hummer with a full gas tank while I farted off in an old puke-green Mercury he used for undercover work. But it ran well once I got started and except for pieces of rotten vinyl flying off the roof occasionally, all seemed well. I had decided to swap since Saul told me Tit was aware of the bureau's interest in the ferry operation.

I smiled as I watched Blaise turn on Princess Street and into the Water Street condo parking lot. I waited for her to go inside before pulling between a red convertible and a sparkling midnight-black Jaguar. I found the right condominium, but that's as far as I went. Well, not exactly. I did get down on the floor and look under the space at the bottom of the door, hoping they didn't snatch it open and trip over me. I needn't have worried. On the other side of the door I saw a blouse, a lace bra, and heels strewn on the floor. I could hear enough to know they weren't going out for a while.

I stayed hidden in the parking lot until they came out and sped off in different directions in their own vehicles. I wanted to check out Trollinger's pad if I could get in. Fortunately he'd forgotten to lock up in his haste to leave. I stepped into the loft with its light oak floor. The room was scantily furnished, but the walls were gorgeous: one with a mural of a huge blue pelican in flight, another cobalt blue with a large sea star mural, and yet another a soothing green with a big conch shell mural. A tall light stood in the corner near a glass-tiled fireplace with no mantel. Two club chairs in blue and white were the only seating, placed near the palatial window that offered a grand view of the Cape Fear River.

A long plain desk housed a computer monitor, the power off, much to my disappointment. I eased over to the master suite. The stunning bed with high scrolled mahogany head and footboards, plumped with generous dark leather, displayed twisted satin bedding, smells of sex lingering in its folds.

I didn't find anything I could use against Trollinger, but I'd learned where he lived, and I'd confirmed that he, still in his twenties and forty-something Blaise were a hot item. I had to wonder where this left Antonella, or if she even cared.

I headed for the new townhouse where Antonella had moved.

"You again?" Antonella stomped back into the room, huffing with anger. "You keep following me. Why aren't you out finding Maeve's killer?"

"I didn't know you cared."

"Wh..what? Of course I care, Agent Hunter." Tears oozed to the edge of her eyes and then slid down her cheeks. "Nobody should die that way."

"You haven't seemed too interested. Anyway, I'm still investigating. You know, *Fearsome Ferry,* The Flash Van, and, of course, numerous porn sites. You've already admitted to being into phone sex and recruiting people for the ferry. Quit playing the innocent bystander. And that's not the worst of it, is it?"

"What are you talking about?" she screamed at me.

"Your mother, Antonella. She's up to her ta-tas in the porn business. And she's over at Trollinger's loft right now screwing his balls off."

"No! You're lying!"

"Stop the act."

"No, no, it can't be true. You're trying to hurt me. My mom would never... My mom's a respectable businesswoman. She's at a meeting at Wrightsville Beach."

I stared at her. "Are you telling me you don't know about this? You don't know your mother and Trollinger are lovers as well as business partners? And you honestly think she's respectable? My guess is she's the major investor."

Antonella blinked at me with glassy hurt eyes, shaking her head from side to side.

"That bitch!" She threw a vase. "That bastard!" She cleared the table, glass breaking into shards on the tile floor.

My work here was done, the stage set.

25

With my tracking device, I followed the ferry away from the private dock. I again drove roads as close to the river as possible. Chase was in another location, keeping track of it. Then the *dot-beep* stopped altogether. I pulled off the road and waited. Chase texted the message: *Corncake/FF*. If the ferry had moved down the river and out into Corncake Inlet between Fort Fisher and Southport far from any landmass, the only way to get to it was with another ferry or catamaran.

Even with high-powered Bushnells, I couldn't spot the porn palace from a sand dune covered in sea grass. I ate a blueberry Nutri-Grain bar with a bottle of warm water and waited for more information. At nine o'clock, daylight faded fast and I dozed until my *dot-beep* woke me. The ferry moved in my direction, heading to a different dock at two in the morning. I sat in darkness, watching the crew tie up and passengers stroll or stumble off and proceed to transportation that, I supposed, delivered them to homes or private vehicles. I wondered how many of them woke up the next day not even aware of all they'd done to their bodies the night before. And yet, they were repeat and willing clientele of the porn ferry.

I recognized Antonella walking off arm-in-arm with some guy toting a dim flashlight. She wore white micro shorts and a turquoise kurta I could see through. Nothing under it, that much I could tell.

And Chase hadn't responded to my last text.

26

Logan, I'm sorry I…disappeared without…getting in touch…but we've got another one." Chase's words broke up on the phone.

"Chase, your cell is cutting out. I can barely understand you."

"Not cell. Attack…"

"An asthma attack? Chase—"

"Listen. Dead girl."

"Another dead girl?"

"Yep."

"Where?"

"Greensboro. UNCG student. Some…workers found her behind…convention center. Her mouth…duct taped…stuffed with wads of…foil. I suppose to keep noise down during S and M, and my guess…she sucked down…windpipe…stopped breathing. That's what…coroner thinks…not official yet. Could be…accidental."

"Nude?"

"Black leather thong…leather straps went…around her torso and looped through rings…pierced in her nipples. I think she was into rough stuff."

"Chase, are you using your inhaler?"

"Yeah. It just takes a few…minutes to settle me down. Don't worry so much."

"I do."

"I know, babe…and I love you for it." A short silence. "Ahhh. I felt like I was breathing through a stopped-up straw, but I'm fine now."

Until next time.

"Do you think there's a link between her and the other girls?"

"Don't know yet."

"Chase, I'm positive now that Tit, uh, Thomas Irving Trollinger, is running the show down here."

"Perfect name for a porn operator."

"Yeah. We can shut him down any time we want to, but there's a girl missing. In fact, Pepper's fiancé's daughter."

"Whoa! Pepper has a fiancé? Boy, am I behind."

"Soon to be former fiancé if I have my way. It's a long story. I haven't had a chance to tell you. It's not like we spend any chat time together."

"I know, honey, but when this case is over we'll slip off on that honeymoon." I nodded but said nothing. "You think Tit has anything to do with this missing girl?"

"Well, Laila is a grown woman but may be emotionally unstable. Tit seems to be a smooth operator and apparently has a temper, but I can't prove he's a murderer—at least, not yet—and of course, we don't know that this particular woman has come to any harm. According to her father, she disappeared on her own and is rebellious enough to stay hidden if that's what she wants to do."

"Do you think it's time to bring this guy in for questioning?"

"That's my intention, but I'm checking out his sleazebag webmaster, Rudd Roache first. They call him Rude. He looks like a psycho."

"Well, we both know you can't always go by looks."

"And Turrentine also has a retarded son down here. I think he might be the one who attacked me."

"When were you attacked? Jesus, Logan!"

Oops! I hadn't told him about that, had I?

I needed to change the subject quickly. "Are you whispering for some reason?"

"Just got a little congestion. Logan, I'm fine. Stop worrying."

~~~~~

I spent the next morning figuring out Rude's snake hole in the back room of ePress, a deserted brick-and-mortar newspaper office building downtown. I busted into the back and had my gun to his temple before he could bolt.

"Rudd Roache, you're under arrest for distribution of underage pornographic material."

"What?" He tried to get up and I slammed him down hard in the chair, slapped cuffs on him, and yanked him to his feet. He spit at me with his disgusting mouth, a gesture I abhor. He left me no choice but to slam his head into the doorframe on our way out. I took my time looking around while I waited for backup. McCracken was some backup. Never around when I needed him.

To my delight, Chase suddenly filled the door. We grinned at each other.

"She's roughing me up, man! Get this bitch off me!"

Chase got in Rude's face. "You call Agent Hunter a bitch again and you'll be unconscious."

"You can't hold me. I'll be out in an hour," Rude bragged. "It's not underage porn. Every one of our clients signed a form stating they were over eighteen and consenting. You can't touch me!"

"We know for a fact some girls are under eighteen. And Trollinger's been telling some of his clients, as you call them, if we got close, he'd sacrifice you since you're the webmaster," I lied. "So, you're going down."

"You're lying! Tit and I are partners." His face reddened as he admitted too much.

"Even partners want to save their own skins. It's your name behind the scenes of the web stuff, not his. He may be able to wiggle out, but you can't." I got down to eye level with the shit face. "You see, Agent Railey here's a techie too. He knew how to track you down, didn't you, Agent Railey?" I winked at Chase.

"That's right, Roache. I've got all your historical data. I know exactly what's on all your porn sites."

"All of them?" Rude looked at Chase in disbelief and I wondered how many more sites were yet uncovered. "Even Gay Skies?"

"Yep, even Gay Skies," Chase answered while looking at me quizzically. I shrugged. Chase shut down computers and prepared to disconnect each so we could confiscate them along with hundreds of disks, CDs, and boxes of pornographic pictures. I found seven digital cameras, all containing saved pictures that would have been shared with the universe eventually.

As I yanked Rude through another door, he planted his feet and tried to wrestle out of my hands. He got quiet once I twisted the cuffs almost enough to tear both shoulders out of their sockets.

"You're a pipsqueak. I can handle you with one hand, shit face, so you might as well resign yourself to going to the cooler," I said using my ugliest tone.

"I'm just the webmaster! I don't even take the pictures. This isn't my operation. You've got the wrong guy!"

"We plan to bring down the whole operation, Roache. Even though Trollinger's willing to give you to us, you're remaining loyal to him. That's mighty nice of you."

"Tit ratted me out?"

"Your name came up in a conversation."

"I don't believe you. You're lying!"

"We've found the bodies of several college girls around the country, mainly here in North Carolina. They're all linked to your sites or one of the vehicles you use for porn. The way I figure it, you and Trollinger use people, abuse them, and dump them. If they cause trouble, you whack them." I was way out of line, but couldn't stop myself. Even Chase gave me an awkward look.

"No! Yes, we're into porn, big time, but we're not killers. You gotta believe me." It was difficult to believe a face that resembled the backside of an old withered hyena.

We moved Roache to Chase's dark blue Marquise. "You have the right to remain silent. If you give up that right, anything you say can and will be used against you in a court of law." Rude had been silenced, but I doubted my murder charge would stick.

McCracken finally showed up and we finished getting Rude's computer equipment and disks collected for evidence. I sat at the desk while he disconnected wires from underneath and tied them together as a man approached.

"Agent Hunter? I'm Channing Caudill, technician from the Federal Building on Water Street." I shook his hand as McCracken backed out of his hole.

"Caudill, I'm glad you could come over. We're confused about how this stuff works."

McCracken interrupted, "I'm taking this stuff and clearing out."

I made no comment and kept my attention on the technician.

"Please call me Channing. It's less intimidating for me."
I nodded. "You're after *Fearsome Ferry?*"

"Yes. You know it?"

"Only by hearsay, I assure you."

"I don't understand how *Fearsome Ferry* lets certain people know where they are. They move it constantly."

"I have a theory, but I must admit I'm not sure about it," Channing said. "Anyway, here goes: everybody's got a cell phone with texting—they call it 'sexting' when they use it to meet for sex, and, of course, as you're aware, byteheads invented web-browsing anonymity."

"I thought sexting was when a kid posed nude and sent it out on the World Wide Web."

"Sexting can be lewd pictures taken and sent by cell phone or on computer. It can also be any sexually explicit message. I suppose this kind of group just borrowed the name."

"It's still a felony charge," I said, taking notes in my PDA. "Okay, back to the anonymity issue. How does it work?"

"Let's say the designated bytehead goes to a library, maybe UNCW Library—if he's a student there—or New Hanover County Library, right around the corner from here, or even Hampstead. Thing is, he has to change locations to stay virtually untraceable."

"There are only so many libraries," I said.

"True, but coffee shops are all over the place and they have Wi-Fi. The geek sets up an account with bogus ID and saves a draft message. If certain people know the account login information, they can read a draft without having to send or receive any message. Byteheads use encryption all the time."

"There must be a way to break into the system and identify the user. Hackers do it all the time, don't they?"

"Unlike hackers who want to destroy the entire hard drive, these guys just want to swim in the sewer and run under the radar," Channing explained.

"Okay, so they cover it well. How do they get the people to certain locations?"

"I'm stabbing in the dark here, but I guess they trusted 'guests' or clients who've been on the ferry or van, so they give out their cell numbers and secret instructions on how to reconnect. This is just my sketchy theory, mind you," he added. "I asked Eliece Booker to add her perspective."

"Another expert?"

"Yeah. She's more knowledgeable about anonymity than I am."

"Okay. Good." I glanced around but saw no one. "They may be threatening folks to keep them quiet."

"Could be, but the technician may create an email for the porn lover's address book, describe activity and location, and ask this select group to forward information to interested friends, or better yet, tell them by word of mouth without forwarding. That would be smarter and safer for them."

"From somewhere like a library or coffee shop."

"Right. Like I said, they can't go there but once. They may bounce around all kinds of shops and businesses where they can gain access. I'm sure they have rules about not displaying a link to the blog or draft—if that's even how they communicate. The guy sends links to the blog with different instructions each time. After a certain length of time, he removes the link and emails them not to go back to that particular blog."

"Clever."

A young woman appeared beside Channing. "I'm sorry it took me so long. Wilmington traffic is horrible this time of day." She thrust her hand toward me. "I'm Eliece Booker."

Channing Caudill gave her a slight hug and filled her in on what he had told us before we got to the same questions I'd asked him.

"What Channing told you sounds fairly reasonable but that's certainly complicated for someone to operate."

"What's your theory?"

"Based on what y'all have told me, I'd be willing to bet the masterminds behind this operation bought a URL from a foreign country, maybe Poland."

"Poland?"

Channing scratched his head. "Details, please."

"Okay, I'm guessing at Poland as a source because even though the URL must be registered and purchased, they're liberal, only requiring a short description of why you should be granted a certain name. Anyone can blow through that in seconds. Once the URL is purchased, the site adds RSS feed which sends a notification by a reader service or email to guests, telling them the site's been updated."

Channing took all this in. "Her theory beats mine by a mile, Agent Hunter."

Eliece smiled. "Now the feed may list several articles that have been updated. Let's say three, for our purposes. Then the third hyperlink should be clicked on. That links guests to a proxy that allows them to type in the URL of the site with the ferry's location."

"Sophisticated operation," I said.

"Absolutely, and as long as there are no meta tags and the address isn't a real word, it won't be picked up by search engines, especially if it's a pl domain or something similar."

"So *Fearsome Ferry* might use something like *ff.info.pl* and nobody would be the wiser?"

"Yep."

Channing used his stylus for a second and shook his head. "Well, that's not it, but I think Eliece is on the right track."

"Domain names can be as long as sixty-three characters too. Don't forget that."

"*Fearsome Ferry* does have its own web site full of porn, but this certainly makes sense for providing their customers with ferry locations."

"I can tell you this, Agent Hunter," Eliece concluded, "these people are highly intelligent and unscrupulous, and this is one of the most sophisticated operations I've run into. The web site will have directions to ferry locations and maybe codes for activities. They update daily, weekly, or whenever. Since there're no tracking cookies on this kind of site, there's no trail for law enforcement to follow. I wish y'all plenty of luck uncovering it."

"I'm sure we'll need it."

"Porn is rampant. I worked on a case where a policeman got fired when pictures of his naked wife surfaced on a porn site."

"Did he take them?"

"Worse than that: he owned the porn site they were on."

"Is it easy to start your own business?"

"Far too easy. Pornography doesn't just involve pedophiles and kids, Agent Hunter. I'm sure you're aware that millions of adults participate on every conceivable level."

Aware, but I somehow had trouble taking it all in. I thanked the two technical experts for a much better understanding of how *Fearsome Ferry* continued to operate successfully.

When I finished at Roache's office I strode toward a man wearing a shirt tied into a halter over his hairless chest.

"Hey, what's up?"

I started to walk away. "Mind your own business."

"So that's the thanks I get for putting clues under your windshield? Well, piss fire!"

I whirled around. "You did that?"

He gave me a haughty sneer and started walking in the opposite direction, clicking his women's heels. I ran after him, catching his arm and causing him to scrape his knees on the brick street as he went down. He crawled up and sat on wood decking near the river. I sat down beside the pathetic, whimpering man.

"Look, I didn't mean for you to get hurt. I just want to talk to you."

"Yeah, now you do, don't you, Antibiotic?"

"I'm Logan Hunter, SBI. I'm not familiar with that term you're using, but it doesn't sound very respectful."

"It means bitch," he said with a grimace.

"Okay. I guess I deserve that."

He looked up at me, wiped his face, and threw out his hand. "Romulus Cocker. I'm sorry to be a crayola, but—"

"Wait. I don't understand your language."

"Oh, sorry. It's gay speak. I'm a crayola. It means I'm highly emotional." He grabbed his barely scraped knee. "It hurts." He rubbed both knees and looked at me.

"Well, in order for me to understand, you need to speak straight English because I'm not gay."

"Okay."

"Mr. Cocker, you said you put the paper under my windshield with *Fearsome Ferry* porn site. Why?"

"And the van site too. I'd figured out you were an agent. You're after Tit, and I want him to burn in Hades. I want you to take him down, Agent Hunter."

"Maybe I can with your help. Come on, let's get your knees cleaned up and get a burger. I'm starved!"

He hopped to his feet and glided with no visible limp toward the parking lot. He had no car, so I offered him a ride in the Hummer, which delighted him. We caught up with Chase at Tomatoz on College Road. He said Rude had called Tit to get him a lawyer.

I introduced Chase to Romulus, who promptly sat down on Chase's side of the booth, leaving me alone on the other side. Chase's face turned beet red as Romulus winked at him.

"Chase, Romulus might be able to help us."

Chase gave me a questioning look.

"Romulus, this is Agent Railey, SBI."

"Wow SBI. I feel so...so, um—"

"Honored?" Chase smirked.

"Yeah, honored." He picked at a burger while I asked questions. "Romulus, why do you want Tommy Trollinger punished?"

"Yum, I haven't eaten in days." He took a huge bite and talked with his prissy mouth full. "Tit is an Anaconda. I used to be a regular on The Gay Skies until he kicked me off."

"Wait. Remember what I said about losing the gay speak? What's an Anaconda?"

"A traitor. He let me on the plane and then threw me off as soon as we landed one night. He told me not to ever try to get on again."

"A gay porn plane?"

"Yeah, nothing but kangkang for the gays and lesbians, those with plenty of money who want to do it in the air. Oh, it's the best kangkang I ever had!" He grew louder and I shushed him as eyes glared at us from around the diner.

Chase had backed his shoulders up the side of the restaurant wall as far from Romulus as possible. "What the hell's kangkang?"

"Sex, man. The most glorious sex you can ever imagine! I could make an X-man outta you, you gorgeous hunk of male."

Eyes stared and mouths gaped open in shock.

"Get the hell up! Let me out of this booth right now!" Chase shoved Romulus, who hopped up and swung a hip.

"Yeah," I said. "We've overstayed our welcome here anyway."

"Listen, Va-Jay-Jay, I—"

"Look, I don't know what you're calling Agent Hunter," Chase had Cocker by the neck, "but it doesn't sound gracious. I hear anything other than Agent Hunter, I'm cleaning your clock, got it?"

"Oh, I love a rough man!"

Chase's fist caught Romulus off guard, knocking him to the sidewalk right outside the diner. He curled into a fetal position and cried like a baby while patrons gaped out windows.

"SBI. We've got everything under control." I'm sure it didn't look that way so I flashed my badge at them and walked over with folded arms and looked down at the sickening heap of flesh on the cement. If I were not getting good information from Romulus, I'd have kicked him in the peas. I reached out to him and he slowly got up.

"I don't suppose it would do me any good to file assault charges," he sniffed.

"You said you like it rough," Chase said over my shoulder, begging for more.

"Guys, knock if off! We've got to work together. No more fighting. And, Romulus, I swear I'll personally shoot you in the ass with a hollow point if you don't stop with the gayspeak. It's disrespectful and I won't tolerate it!"

Romulus Cocker bowed his head. "I'm sorry I called you a vagina."

"Apology accepted. I think. Now, let's get busy. I want Tit as much as you do."

Chase and I pulled an all-nighter to get all the details we could from Cocker, then lose him. He gave us good information on where to find the porn plane and its crew. We passed that information on to the airport authority since we had our hands full enough.

27

Rude got out on bail before the next morning, his attorney stating that all "web stars" were consenting adults and signed forms verifying their ages and willingness to participate. Still, I knew false IDs were easy to come by and some web stars had obviously lied about their ages. I also found no system in place to authenticate information each star had given. But I had bigger fish to fry at the moment.

I could see the three-story house before I turned into the gated community of Landfall and showed my ID to the guard. The house with white trim had enough white porches and balconies to be a beach-resort hotel instead of a family home.

I parked on the edge of the driveway and followed a sidewalk through some shrubs to the front white gate. I unlatched it and walked up to the massive glass front door. Perhaps Blaise Beaujue-Dufour had found this place and kept it for herself. Who could blame her? And if she were a designer, I could hardly wait to see the interior—if she let me in.

A maid came to the door.

I showed her my badge. "Good afternoon. I'm here to see Ms. Beaujue-Dufour."

The maid didn't appear the least bit surprised or impressed. "Right this way, ma'am."

I followed the petite lady inside, glancing up at the three-story cathedral foyer and the chandelier, if you could call it that: modern, with many glass blades that played with light and forced it through to the next blade, huge enough to light up the tall space, even though palatial third-story French doors did their share. I followed her through a bright gold dining room, a real showstopper.

"I would never have thought to put gold and bright yellow together," I said out loud.

"It is quite cheerful, isn't it?" The Caucasian lady was polite and articulate.

Oh yeah. An understatement. And it didn't seem to fit Blaise Beaujue-Dufour's personality, but maybe I brought out the worst in her. Shiny hardwood floors along with gold walls and a yellow table, chairs and a topiary privacy screen left me wondering if they were yellow or a light oak. In the center of the table a two-foot green vase stuffed with roses and fronds of white flowers looked like huge clumps of baby's breath, but weren't. Place settings for two caught my eye.

The maid led me into the kitchen. "Please excuse the mess. I've just come in from the market."

Three cloth shopping bags sat on the long island near a built-in wine cooler, three more on the hardwood floor, and one on a white bar stool. This room had walls and cabinets of white along with an industrial-size stove. On a window shelf sat three white ceramic monkeys—See No Evil, Hear No Evil, and Speak No Evil—along with a couple of lush potted plants. On the other side of the room a grooved shelf displayed six blue plates, each with a different animal picture and the French word for it underneath. We walked out into a courtyard behind the home. A white hammock with exquisite crocheted lace and tassels nestled near some flowering shrubs and a stone wall, the perfect spot to watch yachts sailing down the Intracoastal Waterway.

I could hear loud voices as I continued to follow the housekeeper onto the terrazzo patio near a pool. I approached Antonella and her mother, never taking my eyes off them. They were discussing Tommy Trollinger. I thanked the maid, asked her not to introduce me, and I'd take it from here. She hesitated before disappearing into the house with a shrug. I stood and eavesdropped on the quarrel.

"How could you, Mother?"

"Listen, get a grip! Do you want the neighbors to hear us?"

"You're worried about neighbors? At this point I don't give a damn. Mother. Tit is twenty-two, for crying out loud. You're forty-five—"

"Forty-four," Blaise corrected, as if one year made any difference. "Look, we're business partners. He's a good-looking guy. One thing just led to another. And stop calling him Tit. His name is Tommy."

"Agent Hunter was right."

"Agent Hunter?"

"She told me you and Tit were tight and she thought you were a major investor, at the very least."

"Well, Agent Hunter doesn't know everything," Blaise snorted. "Get over it, Antonella. We're not having this conversation again. It's not like you're Miss Goody Clean Crotch."

My cue to step around the shrub. "Good morning, ladies. Nice day, isn't it?"

"Agent Hunter?" Antonella seemed relieved. Her mother looked hostile.

"How did you get in?" Ms. Beaujue-Dufour howled at me.

"Your housekeeper. She apologized for the boisterous behavior out here."

"Well, she'll be apologizing someplace else from now on."

"Leave Sabrina alone, Mother. It's not her fault we fight."

"Ladies, we need to talk."

Blaise started toward her house. "You can talk to my attorney. I've had quite enough of your harassment, Agent Hunter!"

"Investigating murders of several college students does not constitute harassment, as I've explained previously."

"Several murders?" I had Blaise's attention. She looked at her daughter.

"Mother, are you mixed up in murder?"

"Certainly not, Antonella! How dare you think such a thing!"

"Ladies, ladies, please. Rest whatever it is going on between you long enough for me to state my business, and then I'll leave you two to hash it out."

"Sabrina! Sabrina!" The housekeeper appeared in the doorway. "Bring us three lemonades. With a bottle of vodka," barked Blaise.

"Please," Antonella added. I smiled as Blaise glared at her daughter for correcting her in front of me.

"Well, Agent Hunter, I suppose you think I'm a despicable mother."

"Oh, Mother," Antonella said, rolling her eyes.

"Ladies, we can do this downtown if you won't cooperate." I gave them both the most evil eyes I could force. "You see, I truly don't give a shit what's going on between you two. But you're both involved in the porn business and you will cooperate or go to jail."

Antonella squirmed. "But I haven't—"

"Save it, Antonella. I won't listen to any more of your lies. I've seen you coming off *Fearsome Ferry* with men and nothing on but a see-through kurta. You're very willing to board, knowing what happens there." She blushed in silence.

"When, Antonella?" Blaise snarled.

"Oh, are you concerned about your daughter, Ms. Beaujue-Dufour? I've seen you smothering Trollinger with kisses in his convertible and at his residence."

"You've been to Tommy's?"

"I'm aware you're a partner and a financial source behind the huge operation. We know about *The Flash Van* and the gay plane too. We're pulling the plug on your abominable industry. Dead girls around the state are all connected to at least one of your porn vehicles."

Blaise dropped into the nearest chair.

"I swear to you, I'm not involved in murder, Agent Hunter. Neither is Antonella. I can't imagine that Tommy is either. You're looking at the wrong people. Try Rudd, the webmaster."

"He's already been taken into custody one time."

"Tommy too?"

"Not yet, Ms. Beaujue-Dufour. That's where you come in. We need your help to find out if he's the murderer or if he's contracting a killer to do his dirty laundry."

"This doesn't sound like Tommy. True, he's a genius, mature far beyond his years. He found an easy way to make millions. Girls are going to frolic one way or another. Why not take advantage of it? But murder? No, he wouldn't hurt anyone."

"It's certainly nice of you to be so willing to defend him after he made you a porn web star too."

"Wh..what?"

"Oh, I'm sure you're aware that you're on at least one of the web sites—"

"No!" The color abandoned Blaise's face. "What are you suggesting?"

"I'm not suggesting. I've seen you with my own eyes—
along with millions of other people—having sex online."

"That's impossible!"

"Mother!"

"Antonella, this…this woman…this agent…is lying!
She's trying to trick us into turning on Tommy." She
scampered to the back door. "I'm calling Roland Miller, my
attorney, right now. Antonella, not another word!"

"Suit yourself, Ms. Beaujue-Dufour. He can watch the
video with us." I couldn't help myself. She froze and then
started back toward me.

"I want to see it. You show me the site right this minute!"

"I'd be glad to." We all went inside and I sat down at
Blaise's computer and typed in the URL. When the site
loaded, it offered lurkers several options. I clicked on "Older
Whores" and the screen filled. Blaise was the homepage
feature of the week.

"Oh my God!" Blaise screamed. "I'll kill him!" Her fists
clenched and her face reddened. Antonella paled and backed
away from her mother.

"Ms. Beaujue-Dufour, I have a better solution."

28

"Agent Hunter?"

The voice came from my back seat at the same time I felt the gun between my shoulder blades. I forgot to look before I got in. How stupid.

"We need to talk," Tommy Trollinger said in a calm voice. "Pull over there under the streetlight. I don't mean you any harm."

I hit the gas and then slammed my brakes hard enough to throw him off balance. He flipped over the console into the front seat beside me, his head in the floor, feet over the back seat. I stuck the pistol I yanked from my ankle pocket firmly between his sizable gonads and cut the Hummer's engine.

"It's not a gun!" He looked at me upside down from the floorboard. I reached down and picked up the bamboo stick he'd used to fool me. "Can I get up before I pass out?"

"Move carefully, Mr. Trollinger. Pull yourself back over the seat, then step out and get in the front seat like a nice boy, unless you want to lose your manhood." He did as I instructed, his face sullen, my gun aimed at his head.

"Why did you make me think you had a gun?"

"You wouldn't give me a chance to talk otherwise," he said. "I know you've uncovered the porn ops and you confiscated most of Rude's stuff. I know you've talked to Blaise and know she's involved. But I swear to you, Agent Hunter, we haven't killed anybody."

So Blaise couldn't keep her frigging mouth shut even after being betrayed. "I wish I could believe that, but everybody we question has connections to one of your moving porn establishments or at least one of the web sites. It didn't take much effort to uncover your enterprises since you're extremely brazen."

"Yeah, well, I can't explain why dead girls are connected to any of my stuff. Please believe me."

"Why should I?"

"Because I'm innocent."

"That's what they all say."

"Okay then. What if I help you catch the killer? It's bad for my business."

"Do you know who's killing them?"

"No, but maybe we can lay a trap or something. I'm game." Trollinger turned to face me. "Look, I can shut down web sites, stop the vans, ferry, and plane for a while and have no money worries for a long time, but if the killer's finding his victims online, or on one of my vehicles, wouldn't it be better to leave things up and running and set a trap?"

"You've given this some thought."

"Not so much until I talked to Blaise and Rude. I mean, I've been concerned about the murders but really didn't think they had anything to do with us."

"Trust me, they do."

"How can I help?"

I moved the pistol to my lap. "I need to think about it and talk it over with my partner."

"Okay. Does that mean I can go?"

"No, I have a question for you. Are all your girls legal?"

"They sign a form stating they're at least eighteen."

I looked at him sideways.

"Look, we don't ask them to present birth certificates, okay? But you'd be surprised how many girls look underage with the right makeup. Some men prefer that look, even if the girl is in her mid-twenties and very experienced."

"How did you get started in this business?"

"All around me were girls and grown women willing to do anything at parties, raves, out on the street, you name it—without any promise of money. They're wild. And give them a couple of drinks, and *whamo*! They'll do anything you want them to."

I knew he told the truth about how willing some of them were. "And made more willing when you drop GHB into their drinks."

"No! I've never done that. I don't have to drug them. They're hot to trot."

I didn't believe him and his eyes easily gave him away.

"How well did you know Maeve Smoltz?"

"Too well. She was shy and cute to begin with, but she got cocky. I called her an attention whore; she'd do anything, and I mean, *anything*, for attention. She spread like strawberry jam for anybody. Maeve loved excitement and danger and threw herself at me and lots of other guys all the time.

"The night she died, she'd begged me to have sex with her and I told her to meet me at a dark place on campus just to get away from her." He looked at his hands, wringing in his lap. "Then I just didn't show up. I had no intention of showing up. She had turned into a garbage collector. I'm sure she was loaded with STDs."

"Am I supposed to believe that you're selective after what I've seen on your web sites?"

"Agent Hunter, I swear to you, I didn't set her up. I *stood* her up. But I do feel somewhat responsible for her death. If she hadn't gone out to meet me, she might still be alive."

"Could someone have heard you setting up the date with her and showed up in case you didn't?"

"I suppose so, but it's more likely that she told people. She liked to brag."

"What time were you supposed to meet her?"

"Nine o'clock."

The coroner had placed Maeve's death between nine o'clock and one in the morning.

"And where were you instead?"

"On the ferry."

"What time did you board the ferry and where did it go?"

"On that particular night I boarded by 7:30. I didn't want her to come looking for me. We took a big party out and came in after two in the morning."

"Location?"

"Uh…" he didn't want to tell me all his secrets. "Do I have to divulge that?"

"Well, it seems to me that unless you were far away, you could have killed her and eased on board late without any witnesses. After all, it's your operation. Who'd say anything?"

"I didn't ease on later." He let out a seismic grunt. "Okay, on the night in question we docked down River Road and went to Carolina Beach Inlet after we picked up passengers. We stayed offshore. Rude and the rest of the crew can account for my whereabouts."

"Like I would trust Rude to tell the truth," I said with disgust. "He would lie for you in a heartbeat."

29

Chase, McCracken, and I met at The Goody Goody Omelet House on Market Street about dark. I swilled a Pepsi while I waited for my loaded omelet to arrive and McCracken filled us in on what he'd learned in the past few hours.

"Just as we all suspected, there are a couple officers who seem to be on the take. Don't have names yet, but one's Brunswick County and the other New Hanover. We think they're on water patrol. They're taking mega pay-offs to react slowly or be tied up somewhere away from the ferry, or to let Trollinger know where the trap is so he can avoid that area on any given night."

"I bet they get paid off with more than money," I said.

"I would imagine so. Like I told you before, the two counties run into plenty of conflicts over who has jurisdiction at certain spots. I guess a few of them figure 'What the hell? I'll profit from all the misunderstandings.'"

"Well, Trollinger was smart to work it that way," Chase added.

"He agreed to help us set a trap for the killer for lesser charges against him. He's coming into the New Hanover substation in about an hour. The lab technician will get DNA samples."

"But, Logan, do you really think we can trust this dude?"

"McCracken, he and Blaise swear they don't murder people. Trollinger as much as told me he'd shut down his operations until this killer is caught."

"And then we all know he'll open right back up," McCracken snapped.

Yes, we knew we couldn't stop the porn industry for long. It wasn't just this porn operation. There were thousands—maybe millions—of other operations all over the world.

McCracken asked, "So what's the plan to close in and end this ass-o-rama, at least for a while?"

"I'll work on a plan with them, but I told Trollinger to leave Roache out of this discussion because he might be a suspect," I said.

"Do you seriously think he'll do that? They're in business together, for Christ's sake!" McCracken wanted a piece of Tit.

"Look, Trollinger's selfish and wants to save his own ass. He'd hand over his own mother not to be associated with murder. And, yes, I'm sure he's already planning to gear up again here or someplace else as soon as this blows over."

"We can wind this crap up a lot sooner with his cooperation," Chase added. "We already got Roache's DNA sample when I booked him before."

"Is there any new information we need to know since Chase has been out of the loop a couple of days?" McCracken, having finished his food and now antsy, seemed ready to bolt.

"Well, Sarah, an agency technician, dug around in Roache's hard drive. She mentioned a database of addresses that were supposed to be inaccessible to anyone but Roache. She cracked it and is sending us a list. She said there were several references to a house at the end of Castle Street here in Wilmington."

"Castle Street?" I tapped Chase's hand. "There's a group home for retarded adults on Castle Street, right at the river's edge. It's called Safe Haven. That's where Pepper's fiancé said his son, Tobias, lives. There's a boat landing too."

"That's it," Crack chimed in. "Mr. Turrentine's the manager. I requested a background check on him." He pulled out his new Blackberry. "Wait. Here it is now." He squinted and began reading the text aloud. "It seems Mr. Turrentine has a criminal record."

"What?"

"Embezzlement, assault on a female, pornography, a real nice guy to operate a group home."

"Well, I'm definitely telling Pepper about Saul now. This can't go on any longer."

"Paul," McCracken corrected.

"What?"

"His name is Paul Turrentine, not Saul."

"But—"

"Twin brothers, Hunter, although they aren't identical."

Twins? Damn! I'm on the backside of this case one more time!

"I remember now. Saul told me his brother ran a group home, but I had no idea they were twins. So the man I've seen boarding *Fearsome Ferry* might be the twin and not Pepper's fiancé?" But I also knew Saul had been on it more than once; he'd confessed as much.

"Either that or they're both involved in the porn on some level," Chase added. "And a bigger question: are these brothers killers?"

We put our heads together and came up with a plan to shut down the porn operations—at least temporarily—and smoke out the killer.

~~~~~

I met Pepper at Mayfaire and we shopped, lunched at Macaroni Grille, and stopped in for a piece of decadent ice cream cake at Cold Stone Creamery. I stuffed myself until I was miserable, and helped her carry the loot she'd bought at The World Market, barely getting it all into her aging Infiniti Q56. She bought most items for her restaurant, with only a few wines and exotic foods going to her house. I didn't buy anything. I just enjoyed watching Pepper, her imaginative wheels turning constantly as she found all kinds of things that excited her.

I bit my tongue several times, wanting to tell her about Saul's complicated and questionable life, but not wanting to give away plans. I did ask her if Saul had a twin brother and she validated what McCracken told me. I hugged her, dreading the time to come when she would hear the inevitable news that her fiancé was a piece of crap. I wasn't surprised that Saul hadn't told her his real story. I'd only give him twenty-four more hours before I took care of it for him.

~~~~~

The next day, Chase was at the Carolina Beach motel nursing another bout of asthma. I wanted to go to him, but he insisted all he needed was some rest and he'd be fine. McCracken and I decided to go on with the plan to use me as bait, but when this case was over, Chase and I were going to have a serious discussion about him taking a desk job until he got his asthma under control.

I attempted to dress like a hooker but I had to wear trousers to hide the weapons I'd have on this particular assignment. I wore uncomfortable heels, even though I knew I couldn't run fast with them on. I hung out downtown while McCracken kept tabs on me in case I needed assistance. I refused to wear a wire so we would communicate by phone, and he promised to keep me in view at all times. I headed to the waterfront to see what kinds of people came out after dark, spotting McCracken, already in position under a shade tree near the river.

As soon as I reached the dock a couple of blocks from McCracken, my cell sputtered.

"Logan! Thank God the call finally went through."

"What's wrong, Pepper?"

"Saul told me not to call you, but you need to help him. He can't handle Toby by himself. When I couldn't reach you right away, I called Chase."

"What are you talking about? Chase is out today from an asthma attack."

"I didn't know."

"Go ahead, Pepper, spit it out!"

"Remember Saul has a retarded son? Well, he's big and mean. He lives in a group home on the river within walking distance of the bridge. Paul, Saul's twin brother, is the manager of Safe Haven."

"Yes, yes, I know all that!"

"He called Saul and told him Toby's got a shotgun and is holding two hostages at Chandler's Wharf. I'm sorry I called Chase. I didn't know what else to do. He's on the way to the scene."

"How long has it been since you called him?"

"At least forty-five minutes. I—"

I crammed the cell in my pocket, noticing that it needed charging, and started running as full speed as my heels would allow toward Ann Street, about six blocks east where The

Pilot House dead-ended at the river in front of Chandler's Wharf. I hoped Pepper or someone had made the 9-1-1 call. I fumbled for my phone.

Where the hell is it?

I had apparently missed my pocket. I could only hope McCracken saw me and had been able to follow me in my haste to get here.

"Oh, no!"

I saw Chase's sedan and Saul's old truck in front of the wharf and people running away from apparent chaos. A shot rang out from inside a shop and I scrambled toward the front door, my Glock ready. I eased the entrance door open a little but saw nothing. With a swift kick and fingers hugging the trigger, I barreled in. I tried to hide the shock on my face when I saw the girl backed up against a jewelry display. I had to look away and then take in the abrasive green skin and dark sunken eyes of the woman I'd seen being raped on the Internet.

"Hurt," she said. I reached for her and she pulled away. I looked in every direction to make sure I wasn't about to be attacked.

"No," she said. Now I could see a mouth full of nasty teeth, brown from dried blood, most of them nubs barely above the gum line. "No," she said, backing deeper into the jewelry store. I quickly scanned it and found no one else. The retarded girl, obviously pulverized many times in the face, fell back on a chair and froze there.

I showed her my badge. "I'm looking for Tobias Turrentine."

She curled into a ball. shaking her head violently.

"Where is he?" Shaking silence. "Look, you need to get out of here. Get outside. There are people who can help you out there." I reached for her emaciated arm. She pulled away again.

"Kill me."

I frantically scanned the store and adjoining shops. "He'll kill you if you stay. Get the hell out of here! Now!"

She scrambled up and ran down the hall while I turned my attention to finding Chase. He had to be in one of these shops somewhere, and so was Tobias.

I stepped to the next shop, Candles and Handles, and saw Saul Turrentine—or was this Paul?—in a pool of blood, his face badly beaten. He appeared to be dead. I moved back out into the main hallway and over to a public restroom door beside the next shop. Nothing but a room in disarray. Moving into a garden shop, I heard a noise and whirled back to the restroom.

"Laila?" I recognized her from the picture—Saul's daughter tied up in a bundle at the end of the counter. I snatched all stall doors open, but nobody hid there. I didn't like being in the confined area, so I reached for her gag. Her eyes bulged and she shook furiously, indicating he was behind me. I spun even before I saw the tall shadow.

"Tobias Turrentine?" One hand held my badge, the other my gun. I inched back toward the hall and away from his sister. He backed up enough to let me. His eyes, set far back in the sockets, were hard to read. He pulled a shotgun up and pointed it directly at me as I stood outside the restroom.

"Geh outta heah!"

"Put the gun down, Toby," I said, hoping the use of his nickname would somehow calm him down. "Do it!"

"Won't!"

"Then we finish this now. You hurt your father. He's dead, Toby. Where's the SBI agent?"

"I din't mean to hurt," came the mumbled response.

"Where's the agent, damn you?"

I took my eyes off this brute long enough to scan for any sign of Chase, feeling more and more panic creep into my body.

An unexpected slap across my head jarred my entire body. My Glock hit a nearby wall and then the floor some distance from me. I lurched for the gun, but powerful arms lifted me with little effort and hauled me backwards through a hallway and outside into the dark mist. The brute continued to drag me.

I had never felt so helpless, so unable to defend myself. He backed me through a nasty alley, in the direction of the riverfront. I fought as much as I could, rested a second, and put up another fight. My shoes dragged the ground but I couldn't swing my knees or feet around to kick him. He was so tall I couldn't head-butt him even with heels on. I never had an opportunity to reach for my ankle holster.

He continued to lug me and I recognized Elijah's seafood restaurant, when we passed it. Where did this big goon plan to take me? It couldn't be good. Did he intend to drown me? With the parking lot pavement ending, I felt grass, my high heels bouncing over it helplessly until one slipped off. I heard sirens, thankful that help was finally on the way.

The huge man breathed heavily now, so I tried to muster enough strength to swing an arm back and pop him in the face. The slap landed on his heaving chest instead, not fazing him. He yanked me hard, and I continued to move backwards against my will until we came to a gravel drive. The gravel bit into my shoeless heel, but I kept looking around, hoping to see Chase or McCracken or to at least get my bearings.

I conserved energy for a few seconds, stopped kicking, and let my legs drop, wrapping one long leg around his leg. With all my might, I kicked my remaining four-inch heel right into his calf.

"Yow!"

He threw me into a doorframe with great force, recovering before I did. The impact stunned me. He snatched my hair and dragged me through a house, past a kitchen, and into a large room. Without turning me loose, he snatched down attic stairs and practically threw me up them, his hand grabbing onto my left leg right above my holster.

He pushed me into the attic, allowing no means of escape. As I flipped onto my side, I realized I'd seen this room before, the room in the rape videos I'd seen online. Breathing became more difficult, but I couldn't let panic win. I had to think clearly. So far this oaf of a man had not uncovered my ankle. I pulled away from him, hoping to get to my weapon before he did, or at least keep him from discovering it until I could gain control. I scrambled up and looked at him.

"It's about damn time you got here with her, you imbecile." A raspy voice shouted from a dark corner, further startling me. The shape moved in front of a bright light, pointing a gun at me.

"Paul Turrentine," I eked out.

"Ah, Agent Hunter, you've done your homework. That doesn't surprise me. I knew you'd soon figure it all out, smart girl like you."

"You killed Saul."

"Wrong. I called Saul and he confronted Toby at Chandler's Wharf." He sighed. "I'm sorry he's dead. And Laila split. I'm sure I'll never see her again."

I eyed the big goon, standing near me in a stupid stupor and then looked back at Paul. "You're raping the clients you're supposed to be looking after."

"Oh, I haven't touched any of them, Agent Hunter. Only Laila, and always consensual. Toby here does the raping. You have to understand that even those with mental disease and erratic hormones have needs just like the rest of us. I simply give them the venue for it."

"Rape is hardly fulfilling a need for a retarded person. You're making millions selling vicious tapes online. You're using these sick people for your own sick needs."

I squinted to see the camera on a tripod before a spotlight blinded me. Paul Turrentine slammed his fist on something hard. "You people have cocked up my whole operation!"

"You killed Maeve Smoltz."

"No. Hold on there! Toby was on his own that time. Off the clock, so to speak," said the cold-blooded videographer. "He overheard her plans, and when the guy stood her up, he took the opportunity—"

"To rape and mutilate her body?"

"Oh, Toby didn't mean to hurt poor sweet Maeve. Ordinarily no man could rape her—so willing, you know. But Toby didn't suit her and when she refused his advances, he got angry, didn't you Toby?"

"And you watched and didn't—"

"And I said you were smart." He slammed his fist on something. "No, Agent Hunter, pay attention!" he yelled, his voice resonating around the attic walls.

"He was alone. When he came home much later and told me what he'd done, we raced over and got her body. There was no time to clean up, unfortunately. What a mess!"

"Why take her all the way to Ev-Henwood to dump her?"

"I, for the life of me, don't know myself, Agent Hunter. I should have just left her there, but I was afraid Toby left incriminating evidence behind. I drove around in the boonies of Brunswick County and when I saw the chained entrance, I thought Maeve would like that spot since the university owns it. She was such wonderful entertainment for those boys over there. We rode around to the lumber road and Toby took her out of the trunk and dumped her. I was surprised you found her so quickly. Such a desolate place."

Both men became more agitated.

"Come on, damn it, Toby! Do her and let's get the hell outta here! Didn't you hear this SBI agent call you retarded?"

"I doin', Mista Paul," Tobias yelled back at the corner. "I'm not tardy!"

As I began to sweat profusely, the huge retarded man stalked me while I circled the room, bumping into a chair, then a rumpled bed. Before I cleared it, he slammed both palms into my chest, knocking me to the bouncy mattress. He pounced on me before I could get up, roll to the side, or reach my pistol, clawing at my shirt as it ripped around my shielding hands like tissue paper, revealing my bra.

Paul Turrentine moaned pleasure from behind the camera as Tobias made sadistic animal sounds. "Yes, that's it."

Sweat soaked me like none I could recall since the rape in high school, those inadequate feelings returning, but my adrenalin and fear kicked in as I walloped Tobias with both arms, kicked with both legs, and screamed. My only scream dissipated into pathetic whimpers once he slapped me, and slugged my jaw with his massive fist. He viciously bit into my neck before tearing off the rest of my clothes.

Still conscious, I stumbled off the bed while he dropped his pants, knowing what would happen if I weren't quick enough. In a daze, without a plan to get past Paul and figure out how to let down the stairs, Toby's swiftness surprised me. He caught my leg before I could get to the attic door, throwing me back toward the bed. Another punch to the jaw stunned me. I could feel my wrists and ankles being tied to the bedposts. Spread-eagle on the bed and terrified by the intensity of his brutality, the realization hit: the brutal rape of an SBI agent would be filmed and on the World Wide Web by morning. No—not an agent—me, Logan Hunter, helpless, defenseless, my pistol holster snapped loose in my torn trousers somewhere. I promised myself never to be in this situation again. Yet—I could hear someone yelling and banging below the attic door.

Crack? Oh, please help me!

Tobias jerked around and headed toward the noise, the spotlight and camera apparently following. As I heard wood breaking and men's voices, I writhed and twisted, unsuccessfully trying to loosen my bound limbs.

After a short scuffle and a gunshot, Crack worked feverishly over my naked body, untying my left hand. I looked into his eyes with tears, but he diverted them to focus on the binding. Just as my hand escaped the rope, Crack jolted up, his eyes wide and shocked before he keeled over onto the floor, a knife in his back.

I saw Toby run to Paul, lying on the floor, apparently shot by Crack. While he cried and shook over Turrentine, I scrambled to untie myself from the other posts. As much as I wanted to look after Crack, I dove instead for my trousers, coming up with my pistol from its holster as Toby again slammed me into a wall, then fled down the stairs and disappeared. I pulled my torn blouse over my head and hopped into my tattered pants, barreling down the stairs, hoping for a shot at the bastard.

The house was eerily quiet. Had he fled or was he going to attack me again any second? I searched this small garage apartment but didn't find anything but blood leading me back toward Chandler's Wharf. I ran barefooted all the way across cracked pavement and sand spurs, having to suck it up. I intended to get this bastard. I approached the entrance door to the shops, listened, and peeked in. No blue lights, no sirens. Where the hell were they?

Tobias stalled in the long hallway, his back up against one of the shop walls, his big chest heaving. We made eye contact. The sensation was like looking a wild animal in the eye. He started to lower the shotgun, then stopped and reversed it to my chest level. His conviction seemed to shrivel to one last hope. I put as much distance between us as possible, my body now in the store's main lobby.

"You ain't takin' me in, you heah?"

He pulled the trigger, making a huge hole in the wall behind me and shattering a display of local art. I backed down the wall away from the glass, trying to keep my eyes on him, hoping Chase would appear behind Tobias at any second, knowing Crack was down for the count.

"Don't make me hurt you, Toby."

He rocked and mumbled before running through a shop and into a small office in the back. I pointed my gun.

Where the hell's backup?

I locked my eyes on Toby's fingers, my own fingers tightly wrapped around my own weapon. I put the laser beam on his forehead as he began to sing, despair washing over his crazed face.

"Oh bewtiful stah of Befwehem…"

I never took my eyes off his fingers, anticipating his next move. When his finger twitched, I shot and rolled as the wall exploded where I'd just stood. I looked back at Tobias Turrentine, the green laser star on his forehead replaced with a dark red hole pouring the life out of him. I could hear the SRT finally barreling through every door in the wharf.

I struggled to move, feeling a strange sensation, a sting that invaded my insides. I glanced down at dark liquid spewing from my left leg. I'd been shot. Two men lifted me into the main shop where I spotted Chase on the floor behind a counter.

"Chase!" I swatted the men away and dragged myself over to him. He was unresponsive, but I felt a weak pulse as other agents and EMTs sprang into action.

"Chase! Hang on! Don't you dare die on me!" I tried to beat the EMT away from me so I could hold on to Chase whose lips had turned blue. I cradled Chase in my arms, sobbing as I scooped up a lot of blood with him.

"Too much blood! Do something!" I hollered at the men.

"Ma'am, that's your blood, not his." Men snatched me away from him as both of us were lifted onto gurneys, some working on my leg and blocking my view of attempts to resuscitate Chase.

"Catatonic. Silent chest," I heard one of them say.

30

They managed to revive Chase twice on the way to New Hanover Regional Medical Center. I tried to get to him, but they pushed me back down until they could wheel Chase through the ER. The doors slammed in front of me as I withered on a gurney and wept, begging them not to knock me out with some drug.

How had our lives unraveled in a matter of minutes, all the plans we'd made evaporated in the blink of an eye? My nostrils filled with the iron smell of my own blood before I passed out.

~~~~~

"Logan?" I recognized Pepper's trembling voice near me, but I couldn't lift my head or speak. My heart cried hysterically, inaudible to everyone else. A nurse dabbed something on my sore jaws, and doctored my neck as I tried to get up. She pushed me back down.

"Ma'am, you can't get up. Just relax and let me take care of these bruises and this bite on your neck." When my eyes filled with tears, she leaned over me. "I'll take you to him as soon as I can, okay?" I think I nodded.

I don't know how long it took my medicated body to move, but as soon as I could, I limped on my bandaged leg to a wheelchair with Pepper's help and she took me to Chase's bedside. I took his IV'ed hand in both of mine. I could hear doctors talking in bits and pieces: ventilator…unresponsive…acute asthma attack.

"He's young and strong. Stubborn. He'll make it, damn it! Don't you dare count him out!" I tried to believe my own words, but the situation looked bleak.

I held my husband's hands in mine again and whispered to him. "You're my hero. My truth. Give me your pain. I can take it. Squeeze my hand, please! I want to hold you close again. I want your kisses. I want you back, you hear me? Please, Chase. Don't die on me. I need you. I can't make it without you. You're my life. Chase, I didn't exist until you walked into my life. Without you I can't survive." Lead tears plopped on my heaving chest. "Oh, God, please don't take him from me."

Time froze.

I could hear Pepper sobbing and talking off in the distance, talking about the ferry and the van, about arresting Tit, Rude, Blaise, and a host of behind-the-scenes people. I disconnected from warped voices in the room, only hearing a distant slow echo. Chase was all that mattered to me. I glanced over my shoulder, and Pepper ran to put both her hands on my shoulders. She stayed with me beside Chase, whimpering and never speaking a word.

When the doctor came in and said that all hope was gone, I buried my head in Chase's chest and sobbed until I was spent. I'm not sure what time I lifted my swollen eyes to the nudge from Pepper. She held out a cup of coffee.

"Logan, this is all my fault. I should never have called Chase. I—"

"No, Pepper."

"Honey—"

"Pepper, I…can't deal with this right now. It can't be over. Chase is strong. You hear of people making it even though doctors have given up on them. It happens every day."

Pepper pulled on my shoulders and gently turned me to face her while my hand held on to Chase's.

"He has irreparable brain damage, honey. Didn't you hear anything the doctors said? He was without oxygen for too long. They said he had brittle asthma and shouldn't have been an agent in the first place. Strenuous exercise and stress triggered it. Oh, Logan, I'm so sorry. I should never have called Chase. I'll never forgive myself."

"I don't believe the doctor." I shook my head, not knowing how to respond to Pepper's guilt-ridden face. "He'll be fine, Pepper. Doctors can be wrong."

"Three doctors have told you the same thing, Logan. Don't you remember? Honey?"

I blinked furiously.

"I feel so responsible. If I just hadn't called him. I should have waited for you to call me back. I—"

"Pepper, it's not your fault!" I yelled in her face. "It's mine. I should have made him go to another doctor. I didn't know he was this fragile." I had said it. Chase was far more fragile than I could have imagined. More fragile than he would admit. Or did he even know how bad the asthma had become? Always on the go, I wasn't sure he took his nebulizer with him on some assignments. The naked truth: Chase didn't take good care of himself because he was too busy taking care of everybody else.

"Did I hear you talking to Crack?"

"McCracken? Yeah."

"I thought he had a knife in his back."

"A nurse rolled him down here in a wheelchair. He's doped up but said the knife missed vital organs. He's going to be okay with some recuperation time." She turned toward me. "Oh, he said police are cleaning up the mess at the group home and Chandler's Wharf. I don't understand why Saul isn't answering his phone. I figured he'd call me as soon as he could."

"Pepper, haven't you heard what happened?"

"All I know is you had to kill Toby because he stabbed McCracken. He would have stabbed you too, Logan."

"No, Pepper." I couldn't get into all the details with her, but she had to know one thing. "Saul is dead."

Her hand flew to her mouth and she began to shake as her eyes filled with tears, but she remained by my side, glancing at me and over at Chase.

"It's a long story, and I just can't—"

"I understand. I'll ask one of the officers in Agent McCracken's room. I'm so sorry for Saul, Logan. I really am, but quite honestly, Saul and I didn't make a good twosome. I planned to break things off with him anyway. He wasn't a bad person, just not right for me. I'm sorry he's dead."

~~~~~

Pepper and I sat quietly beside Chase for a while until a nurse motioned Pepper to the door. When she returned she broke the silence.

"Honey, the doctor says you have to make a decision."

"What kind of decision?" The realization of what she said hit me like a hollow point.

"We've been here by his bed for two days. His condition hasn't changed. You can make the decision, Logan."

"What?"

"You're stronger than anyone I've ever known. You can do…what has to be done." Pepper stifled the words with her own sobs.

Chase's smile. Chase's gorgeous eyes. Chase's touch. *My Chase.* One of God's masterpieces.

"Do you know if he has a living will?"

"We both do." I dry-heaved into a convenient trashcan, sickening hospital smells making me nauseous.

"Pepper, I need Taryn," I whispered weakly. "They have to keep him on life support until a family member says otherwise."

"Logan, *you're* his family. You're his wife." I blinked at her as she gently rubbed the top of my trembling hand. "And Taryn's on the way. I've already called her. She should be here in about an hour."

"Why couldn't it have been me instead of Chase?"

"We don't get to make that decision, honey. I'd gladly take his place so that you two could be together. I'm so sorry I caused this."

"You didn't cause it, Pepper. Chase didn't take care of himself."

We sat stoically until Taryn barreled through the door and wrapped herself around me.

"Logan, you poor baby. I got here as fast as I could throw a few things in a bag." She hugged Pepper briefly and put her arms around me again.

"Taryn, you've got to help me. I don't know what to do."

"What do you need, sugar?"

I glanced at Pepper. "You tell her." Pepper took Taryn by the hand and stepped into the hall far enough away that I could see them but not hear Pepper's guilty hysteria and the doomsday conversation. Taryn nodded several times, and I stopped looking and went back to Chase's side. When they returned, Taryn stood on the other side of Chase's bed, picking up the hand with IV lines and cradling it in hers.

"Logan," her eyes filled with tears. "Chase didn't grow up around me, but I've known of him a long time. We frequented the same diners, and you well know there aren't that many around Trust and Luck to choose from." I nodded. "I have to tell you about a conversation I overheard one day. He sat with another deputy and I ate in a booth behind them, facing Chase. Anyhow, they talked about somebody who had been shot and hooked up to life support." Taryn came around the bed to me. "Logan, he made a statement I think you should know about."

"What?"

"He said 'I wouldn't want to live like that, with no hope of coming out of it. I couldn't stand being a vegetable with somebody feeding me and changing my diaper. Nobody in his right mind would want to live like that.' He meant it, Logan."

So there it was. Taryn had said it out loud. I let out a low cry, sobs flowing, unconscionable pain surfacing with blunt force.

"I know this is terribly difficult, sugar, but nobody wants to live that way. That's not living," Taryn added.

Both friends, crying, hung onto me until we all moved to the hospital window seat for support. A nurse stuck her head in for a second, and then gave us privacy for a few more minutes.

"Taryn, I know you're an organ donor, but I'm not sure I can do that. I'm not sure Chase would want that. We never talked about that, you know?"

"You don't have to donate, but may I say one more thing about that, and then I'll hush."

I could only nod.

"I have strong feelings about donating organs because there are so many people in the world who suffer with every breath, those who were born blind and have never seen this gorgeous world, those who have been terribly burned and live in agony unless skin or tissue donors give them any kind of relief. I could go on and on, but you know how I feel. God has his fingerprints all over you, honey. He'll guide you in making the right decision, but Chase was a generous sweet soul. I ask you this: What do you think Chase would want to do? What would Chase want, Logan?"

I made the toughest decision of my life with Pepper and Taryn by my side. I prayed for God's guidance and strength, my heart broken into a million fragments that could never be mended. Collapsed on the window seat with Taryn and Pepper, I watched as attendants wheeled Chase away from me for the last time, his organs to be donated to others so their lives could be worth living.

McCracken's form filled the door, slumping there with plenty of pain in his own eyes. It was so unlike him to say nothing. Nobody said anything, the silence agonizing. I had to throw up again, this time hoping all pain and hurt would somehow leave my body with the vomit, but knowing it wouldn't be that easy.

The plan: Pepper would drive me to Genesis Beach and Taryn would follow, both staying with me until after Chase's memorial service. SBI agents would make sure Chase's car and my Hummer got home.

I walked out into the last hints of sunset on the worst day of my life, gulped briny air, and sobbed, letting my empty gun slip from my fingers and hit the pavement.

~~~~~

During the emotional weeks that followed, I picked through Chase's personal effects at the Asheville house with Clive nearby. We were both cheerless even though Clive occasionally offered me a cute story of Chase's boyhood and anesthetized my pain for an instant.

"It'll take time to face your loss, Logan," he said, squeezing my hand. I could only nod.

I stayed on at the western house after Clive left for an extended visit to his home in Yorkshire. He promised to return and help me make a decision about keeping the estate. I now had this huge place, the condominium at Genesis Beach, and a primitive cabin near Pisgah Forest. With the love of my life gone, how could I live in any of them?

I cried myself out over the next few weeks. Taryn and Pepper checked on me every few hours but gave me enough space to come to grips with my loss. Taryn brought Homer to stay with me in the house, and I rubbed his ears and tossed him an occasional stick in the large backyard. He didn't wander far, seeming to understand that I hurt and he needed to comfort me.

The front door chime caught me off guard.

"McCracken?"

He wobbled inside with a cane, without my invitation. "I came to see if you need anything. Anything at all."

"Ah. All the way from Wilmington? You could have called."

"I was in the neighborhood. Thought you might want a final report on the investigation."

Before I could stop him, he gave me details. "We got all the evidence we needed to put Trollinger, Roache, and Beaujue-DuFour away for a while. They're guilty of all the porn charges, and Roache had an assault charge, as well as illegal Internet operations tacked on. With the information Beaujue-DuFour gave up once she found out Trollinger had given her an STD and put her on an Older Whores web site, she got a lesser charge. Tit better watch his back though. She'll probably have him killed if she gets a chance.

"Our guys confiscated *Fearsome Ferry* and at least a couple of the vans. Sarah, at central headquarters in Raleigh, found thousands of different girls online, and she's still trying to determine which ones were minors. It'll take a while to identify and track them all down. But Trollinger, Roache, and Beaujue-Dufour were not involved in the killings, Logan."

I shuffled on my cane to the nearest window and stared outside, saying nothing.

"We know Tobias killed Maeve Smoltz. Probably just intended to have sex with her. He'd probably heard some young folks talking about using a Sawzall, but he wasn't smart enough to realize it was supposed to have a dildo over it before he used it on her." He shook his head. "Like using one of those things is normal. Anyway, his prints were on it. We think Paul Turrentine helped him dump her body. There was blood in the trunk of his car. And he almost certainly killed the other women since he set up rapes to film and traveled a lot. He probably nabbed the Glenhouser girl after she auditioned for a movie and brought her to the group home attic where Toby raped her while Turrentine filmed the whole thing. When she fought them, either Toby or Paul killed her. Logan, you were supposed to be next."

I nodded, unable to look him in the eye, wanting to change the subject.

"What about the girl in Boone?"

"Turns out Paul visited Boone about the time she died. And that Tickle girl? This girl from Boone was her cousin. We know they were all in Wilmington from time to time too."

I turned to face McCracken. "My God. Then it all fits together."

"Oh, yeah, and you remember that fag you and Chase questioned?"

"Cocker?"

"Yeah. They found him under the bridge near the group home. His penis had been chopped off and stuffed in his mouth."

"Oh my God! Who would have done such a thing?"

"We're thinking maybe he had a run-in with big Toby. Maybe Toby thought he was a girl. It could happen." I thought about Romulus and how he'd enjoyed his female side to the extreme, but he didn't deserve to die like that.

"What about Saul? I have to know about his involvement with all this."

"We don't think he was actually an investor or really participated beyond what he told you. If anything, he tried to figure it out and take care of it by himself. After all, it was his son and daughter, and his brother. His fatal mistake? Not letting us handle it."

I dipped my head. At least that would be some consolation to Pepper.

"Crack, I'm sorry you got hurt."

"Just doing my job." He winked. "I'm sorry *you* got hurt," pointing his cane at my cane. "If I'd found your shoe sooner, I could have been there to prevent anything from happening, you know. And whoever called SRT told them to go to The Cotton Exchange, not Chandlers' Wharf. They had the damn place surrounded and took their sweet time going through the place before somebody told them the mistake."

"That's why I heard sirens but never saw anyone." I turned away from him. "I don't want to talk about it anymore."

"Then, let's talk about this." Crack pulled something metal from his coat pocket. "I believe this is yours." He presented the gun I'd meant to lose.

I walked away from him. "I don't want it."

"Logan, we need you with the bureau. One of the agents saw you drop it. He brought it to my hospital room." I could hear his cane thumping closer. "Don't give up. Don't let Chase have died in vain."

"What do you know about Chase? What do you know about having to give up the man you love?" I screamed the words at him, turned, and pounded his chest with both fists as tears soaked my shirt. He let me. When I no longer had the energy to strike him, I flopped into a sobbing heap on the floor. He scooped me up on wobbly legs and placed me on the brocade couch before squatting beside me. He winced with watery eyes and stood up, holding his back.

"Oh, but I *do* know about losing a spouse," he said, and I remembered his wife's death—the death for which he would feel responsible for the rest of his life. I suppose we had that much in common. He rose and shuffled to the door, leaving my gun on the foyer table as he disappeared without another word.

I felt bile rising in my throat as I struggled up from the couch and hobbled to the commode once more. I had vomited so much that I felt like the pulp in the reservoir of a juicer—no core left to hold me together.

~~~~~

When nausea hadn't subsided after another month, Taryn piled me in her car and drove me to her doctor's office on Beaucatcher Road. He gave me a complete physical at Taryn's insistence. I had lost weight, was colorless, and had no stamina. I couldn't go back to the SBI like this even if I wanted to.

The doctor came back after I dressed, this time with Taryn beside him.

"I hope you don't mind having your friend here. You might need the support."

Taryn's face showed alarm. I swallowed hard.

"Cancer? I've got cancer?"

"Oh, no, ma'am. It's nothing like that."

"Then what is it?"

"I have great news, Mrs. Railey. You're pregnant!"

Don't miss Susan's upcoming novel,

SLIGHTLY CRACKED

Laugh at the hilarious misadventures of two menopausal women...a virtual menopause in the country! You'll laugh...you'll cry.

Reviews For Susan's Books

Genesis Beach

"...a spine-tingling mystery...Add the Logan Hunter series to your reading list." Lynette Hall Hampton, *Echoes of Mercy*

"...engaging characters, a tight plot and a beautiful, yet unpredictable setting. Pack this one for the beach and enjoy the first book in a promising series." Mary Fran Vesey, *Murder at Treese Family Inn*

"...holds your interest to the very end." Martha Cheves, *Stir, Laugh, Repeat*

"Whitfield crafted an enjoyable mystery filled with vibrant character, capturing the essence of coastal North Carolina." K.R. Jones, *The Ghosts of Guantanamo Bay*

Just North of Luck

"Whitfield takes the reader to the backwoods of North Carolina...[and] weaves a tale that leaves us breathless..." Sylvia Dickey Smith, *Dance on His Grave* and *Deadly Sins-Deadly Secrets*

"...eloquent descriptions of the Blue Ridge Mountains and grisly murders that take place in that beautiful setting will haunt readers." Sunny Frazier, *Fools Rush In*

"Not for the faint of heart." Mark Stevens, *Antler Dust*

"Just North of Luck grabs you by the scruff of the neck and takes you on a harrowing ride from the very beginning… The second book in the Logan Hunter series is a must read." Elise Crawford, *A Promise Kept*

"Quirky characters, humor, and a keen sense of place…" Bob Avery, *Beneath A Buried House*

"Just south of sanity!" Apex Reviews

Hell Swamp

"…a Carolina Low Country tale of greed and misguided deeds. Fasten your seat belt!" Maggie Bishop, *Murder at Blue Falls*

"…Hell Swamp is a good old-fashioned roller coaster ride. Whitfield sprinkles in humorous and colorful descriptions…enough for an occasional chuckle in a tense situation." David Fingerman, *Silent Kill*

"Hell Swamp…riveting from page one, you'll want to read with all the lights on and the doors locked." Teresa Jenner Garrido, *Wind Whisperer*

"The action in Hell Swamp jumps out at you from the first chapter and never lets up. Edgy stuff." Mary Deal, *River Bones*

"…well-written, suspenseful mystery with a likeable protagonist, vivid imagery, a taste of horror, a little tongue-in-cheek humor and even romance. What's not to like?" All Books Review

"Whitfield has drawn a cast of characters from down by the Black River...peculiar, scary and injected with just enough humor to make Hell Swamp stand out from the pack. Read the book. It's a good 'un." Tom Cooke, *Memoirs of Bear*

Killer Recipes

"Don't be afraid to try these concoctions. We only write about murder and poison, we don't participate in them." J.D. Webb, *Smudge*

"Titles are hilarious...recipes are real and delicious. Whitfield has put a fun slant on the old standard cookbook." Mary Deal, *Down To The Needle*

"I'm giving copies to friends for gifts...a worthwhile addition to my cookbook collection." Gayle Wigglesworth, *Mud To Ashes*

Sin Creek

"This action-packed mystery will keep you turning the pages until its shocking end." L.J. Sellers, *The Sex Club* and *Secrets To Die For*

"Lickety-split pace and effective description [in Sin Creek] give the reader the feeling that they are conducting the investigation right along with Logan Hunter. If you're a fan of mysteries, this one is guaranteed not to disappoint. If mystery's not your usual genre, make an exception with Sin Creek. Like the Cyclone at Coney Island, Sin Creek is gripping and intense, yet an enjoyable ride." Mark Rosendorf, *The Rasner Effect*

About Author Susan Whitfield

Award-winning multi-genre author Susan Whitfield is a native of North Carolina, where she sets all of her novels. She is the author of five published mysteries, *Genesis Beach, Just North of Luck, Hell Swamp, Sin Creek and Sticking Point.* She also authored *Killer Recipes*, a unique cookbook that includes recipes from mystery writers around the country. *Slightly Cracked* is her first women's fiction, set in Wayne County where she lives with her husband. Their two sons live nearby with their families.

Susan's a member of Mystery Writers of America, Sisters in Crime, Coastal Carolina Mystery Writers, and North Carolina Writers Network. Her books are available in print and ebook formats. Susan is currently researching a medieval ancestor for an historical mystery. Learn more at www.susanwhitfieldonline.com

www.ingramcontent.com/pod-product-compliance
Lightning Source LLC
Chambersburg PA
CBHW030141180626
46812CB00002B/802